FRIENDLY PERSUASION

As Mark watched Primo, he thought of the oath that every Mafia soldier took: *"La Famiglia Es Il Primo Cosa."* "Family Before All." It was the glue that held the organization together. Mark had to dissolve that glue from Primo's mind.

Mark slapped Primo hard, jolting his head to one side. "How long have you known Tony Rossi? Is Tony really running the family?"

A blank stare.

Mark took out the Beretta. "Primo, how would you like to get shot with your own weapon?" The Mafia soldier shook his head. "No way. Kill me and you'll never make me talk."

"I didn't say anything about *killing* you, just shooting you."

The Penetrator Series:

THE PENETRATOR
BLOODY BOSTON

by Lionel Derrick

PINNACLE BOOKS • NEW YORK CITY

THE PENETRATOR: BLOODY BOSTON

Copyright © 1976 by Pinnacle Books, Inc.

All rights reserved, including the right to reproduce this book or portions thereof in any form.

An original Pinnacle Books edition, published for the first time anywhere.

ISBN: 0-523-00797-3

Special acknowledgments to Chet Cunningham.

First printing, January 1976
Second printing, February 1977

Cover illustration by Mitchell Hooks

Printed in the United States of America

PINNACLE BOOKS, INC.
275 Madison Avenue
New York, N.Y. 10016.

BLOODY BOSTON

PROLOGUE

Mark Hardin sat on the aisle seat of the 747 and enjoyed the view. Three stewardesses in the "no frills" section of the big aircraft moved up and down the aisle talking with passengers, selling quarter drinks of Coke and coffee, and seeming to enjoy not having to rush and scurry carting around meal trays.

The Penetrator winked at the tall redhead, who winked back, then turned and went to the little kitchen forward.

Mark usually flew his Aero Commander, but this time the destination was Boston, and it didn't seem worth the rugged sixteen-hour day of flying. Besides, this wasn't supposed to be a mission. An old school buddy from UCLA had surfaced in Boston. He had been out of sight for three years and at one time was thought dead. Now he had gone to a lot of trouble to

1

track Mark down—most people couldn't find him even when they did try. So Mark had decided to fly to Boston for a couple of days and see what was bothering his old buddy Tony Rossi.

The Penetrator was not a social worker. He specialized in frontal lobotomy surgery with a .45 slug, or an appendectomy removing half the heart as well on those whose violently criminal acts showed they thought they could rape society and get away with it.

Mark Hardin was a one-man assault on crime, corruption, on organized crime and all of its sucking tentacles. He had been jolted into the work when Mafia "persuaders" sent a young girl's car thundering over a cliff, trapping her inside as it burned into a hellish funeral pyre. The death was supposed to be his, and he had vowed to fight big crime and all forms of corruption, graft, and avarice anywhere and everywhere he found it, at home or around the world.

He had gutted a monstrous heroin ring in Los Angeles, shattered a scheme to sell atomic artillery shells to the highest bidder in Japan, stopped cold an attempt to import into the United States virtually undetectable counterfeit currency that could have bankrupted the nation and decimated an attempt by a black power group in New York City to hijack the whole borough of Manhattan and hold it for ransom.

He stared at the redheaded stewardess as she came by again. She grinned and gave him a magazine, a *Playboy*. She laughed and honored him with a sexy little wiggle as she walked away.

The girl's hair reminded him of blood and quickly

he looked at his hands. They were washed clean. *Now* they were clean, he thought. But he often dreamed about blood on his hands. There had been so much. In eleven violent, deadly campaigns he had gambled with his life, and each time he had won, against staggering odds. So far.

The Penetrator tried to relax. They would land in Boston soon. He would see Tony, have a few laughs, some drinks, and then he'd be on the plane back tomorrow night. The professor was working on something in Atlanta. What could happen in Atlanta?

He remembered coming back to the states. He had been shot to hell and stomped into an ugly mass of flesh in Vietnam. As he was recovering, his old UCLA coach had suggested he go talk to an ex-prof from USC who had a little hideaway in the desert near Barstow.

Mark went, and met Professor Willard Haskins, who had built a small wonder inside one of the old borax mines in the Calico mountains. It was almost impossible to spot the place from outside. A garage and small plane hanger had been built into the side of a cliff. Most of the rooms were fashioned from old borax tunnels and the whole thing blended into the surrounding country so well that from the outside you could stumble over a ventilating shaft and never know what it was.

There he had met David Red Eagle, a full-blooded Cheyenne who told Mark he was part Indian. They traced his lineage and found that his mother had been Cheyenne. David Red Eagle began to teach Mark

3

about his heritage as he recovered in both mind and body in the warm desert sun. After the professor's niece was killed in the car crash, Mark vowed to avenge her death on the Los Angeles Mafia, and blasted them halfway to Seattle.

Slowly the three men, Professor Haskins, David Red Eagle, and Mark, decided they should form a triumvirate against crime, with Mark as the action man, David Red Eagle providing training for Mark, as well as Indian lore and techniques, and the professor as the intelligence gatherer.

Mark blinked and looked up. The stewardess was there.

"Sir. You'd better fasten your seat belt; we're about to land."

Mark nodded. She smiled. "I've never seen anyone asleep with his eyes open before."

"It's a trick," Mark said.

She smiled and paused, then smiled again and moved on down the aisle.

Not tonight, Marci, Mark thought. He had to see a man about a problem. But what could the problem be? As he remembered, Tony was the white sheep in the family. His old man was the Boston Mafia. Now what the hell could Tony Rossi want with Mark? He considered a trap, then discounted it. Not Tony. But he was glad he brought along a few of the deadly tools of his trade in his checked baggage. The Mafia had strange ways of reasoning, even with their own.

Chapter One

NARC-ONE GOING DOWN

Carson Beach lay silent, ominous in the darkness all around them. Fragmented clouds rushed across the sky to engulf the full moon. Tendrils of fog drifted off the windswept chop of Old Boston Harbor, gathering on the beach now like some preempting shroud. Nothing moved along the damp sand except the constant wavelets which produced only a sibilant, deadly hissing, as if the ancient goddess Pele were about to erupt in spectacular fury. Here at the very edge of the Atlantic ocean an undefined dread of violence pervaded the scene.

Two men stood facing each other just past the dank wetness of the latest receding wave. Fear set off alarms clanging in the smaller man's mind. He stabbed a glance sideways. There was no chance, no place to run.

Neither man spoke. They stared their bitterness and

5

hatred across the three feet of salt-spray-swept space. It all had been said more than once: the questions, refusals to answer, the sudden move that stripped the smaller man of the weapon that made him as big as anyone—his Beretta automatic.

Mark Hardin's expression never changed as he slammed his big fist hard into the other man's stomach. The powerful blow rocked Archie Primo backward two steps, where he groaned and dropped to his knees. He vomited, then rolled sideways in the sand, drawing up his legs to relieve the knifing pain in his gut. He didn't notice the inch of salt water and foam that surged up the beach and washed past him.

"Primo, if you want to get off this beach alive you'd better start talking."

No reaction came from the man lying in the sand. Mark moved toward him, kicked his toe hard into Primo's side just over his kidney.

"Sit up, Primo!"

There was a snap, a command in the voice that forced Primo out of his pain, compelling him to pull himself up and look at his tormentor.

"We'll start over again, Primo. How long have you known Tony Rossi?"

The man's blank eyes stared upward at Mark, brimming with hatred and contempt, yet with a grudging measure of awe, too. Primo understood violence and what it could do, respected it, used it. But it worked against him now. He remained silent.

"Stand up, Primo."

Again the commanding tone moved the man, as he

struggled to his feet. Mark tested him, taking a slow, boxer-type step forward, leading with a left hand jabbing at the nose. Primo waited until the blow nearly landed, until Mark was committed and extended. Then with remarkable control he ducked the fist, exploding forward, his karate-stiff fingers shooting out like lances, aimed for Mark's stomach and eyes.

The Penetrator expected some attack reaction. Dropping his left forearm from the elbow, Mark turned Primo's midline attack outward, while he swung his right foot in an arc behind his left, pivoting out of the way of the fingers seeking his vulnerable eyes.

Before Primo could recover, Mark chopped sideways, his flat hand slashing hard against Primo's exposed neck. Mark's right hand slanted upward and came down on the bridge of the hoodlum's nose, breaking it in several places, stunning Primo.

The smaller man's knees buckled, but he didn't go down. He tried to get his hands up. But the Penetrator gave him no time, boring in with a pair of solid, hard fists, punishing Primo's soft gut. He slashed a flat right hand against Primo's cheek, bringing a cry of pain. Then Mark powered one more right hand into Primo's soft gut and watched him fold in half and slump backward into four inches of salt water.

Mark caught the man by the back of his sports jacket and dragged him back to the dry sand.

As Mark towed Primo, he thought of the oath that every Mafia soldier took: *"La Famiglia Es Il Primo Cosa."* "Family Before All." It was the glue that held

7

the organization together. Mark had to dissolve that glue from Primo's mind.

He dropped Primo in the dry sand and checked the beach again. There was one lone bonfire, but it was three blocks up the beach. The moon came out fully now and he saw no one along the broad expanse of sand. It was just after midnight.

Mark slapped Primo hard, jolting his head to one side.

"How long have you known Tony Rossi?"

There was no reaction.

"Where are Tony's wife and children?"

Silence.

"Is Tony really running the Family?"

A blank stare.

"Do you want to live for more than ten minutes?"

At last Mark took out the Beretta.

"Primo, how would you like to get shot with your own weapon?"

The Mafia soldier shook his head. "No way. Kill me and you'll never make me talk."

"I didn't say anything about *killing* you, just shooting you."

It brought a flicker of concern to the soldier's face. Mark put away the automatic and dropped to his knees in the sand in front of Primo, backhanding him across the face. It was a diversion. Mark caught Primo's left arm by the wrist and elbow and brought the arm down sharply over his knee the way he broke kindling wood.

Both bones in Primo's forearm snapped. A surging scream roared from the man's throat. It lasted only five seconds before it trailed off, as Primo slumped into the sand, blubbering.

A small muscle in Mark's jaw tightened, then relaxed. There was no room in his mind to pity filth like this. Primo would kill his own sister or father if the Mafia told him to. He was a killing machine, a gun and soul hired in one bargain. But he would talk. Mark would strip raw every nerve in his body until he begged to tell all he knew. They had the rest of the night.

Mark searched Primo with no objection from the Mafioso. In the moonlight he looked at a small gold medallion he took from Primo's pocket. It had three words stamped on the back of it. A Mafia I.D. card, his passport to the Family, and his dog tag if he fell in battle. His wallet contained no addresses. Mark used his pocket pen light and saw the address on his driver's license was smudged and blurred so it couldn't be read. There was over a hundred dollars in the moneyholder. Mark left it there so it would not look like a robbery.

A minute later he caught Primo's chin and lifted his head. "You've had your rest, tough man. How long have you known Tony Rossi?"

"I'll . . . tell . . . nothing." Primo grimaced as he spoke, talking over the pain that ravaged his features.

"I could shake hands with you a couple of times."

"Bastard!"

"I noticed your driver's license has a long expiration date. That means you haven't been here long. Over six months?"

Archie Primo wavered between that euphoric wonderland of semi-consciousness and the surging, blinding, gut-wrenching pain from his arm and nose. The swirls and eddies of agony caught him and swept him hard against massive rocks, doubling, tripling his suffering. Then the mists cleared and he was floating serenely on a placid pond that didn't show a ripple. He tried to relax and let the clear, motionless water claim his body . . . but somehow he couldn't sink.

Then the voice came through, strident, demanding, brutal, asking questions, always questions. With the terrible voice came the drumming of thunderous torment. His arm hurt like hell. Now he was fully conscious again. He blinked at his persecutor.

"Come on, Primo. You know the score. You know damn well that if you want to walk out of here you've got to talk. Otherwise I zap you and let the kids find your body tomorrow."

His eyes caught Mark's. "You sonofabitch!"

"True, but I'm also the guy with the gun. How does it feel on the receiving end?" The Penetrator took out the Beretta. Primo's eyes followed the weapon. Mark sighted in on the man's forehead, then lowered the muzzle toward Primo's navel. "How do you want it, fast or gut slow?"

A chill clouded Primo's concentration. He realized he was as close to death as he had ever been. Dammit, how did he get into a mess like this? Doing what he was told; being a loyal soldier; and what the hell did it get him? He relaxed as the muzzle aimed at a new spot. Primo knew he wasn't going to die. But he wasn't ready for the snarl of his own gun. It came as a mind-blowing shock that sent him scrambling back into the feathery darkness of insensibility.

Mark had shifted the Beretta toward Primo's undamaged arm before he fired. The Model 1951 barked and the 9-mm parabellum slug ripped into the soft side of Primo's elbow, shattering it. The slug broke as it smashed through the bones and the unrelenting lead surged on through flesh, taking bone chips, muscle, and tendons with it as it burst from Primo's elbow in four places, ripping more pieces of flesh away as the lead chunks spent themselves in the sand a dozen feet away.

The small muscle in Mark's chin twitched. His eyes glinted as he watched Primo's blood stain the sand. He moved quickly then, ripping up Primo's shirt, trying to stop the flow of blood. At last he made a tourniquet of cloth and a piece of driftwood, tightening it until the blood slowed to a drip. Mark scooped up a double handful of salt water and threw it in Primo's face, shocking him back to the land of the conscious.

"Now, by God, Primo, we get down to business."

The other man's eyes wavered, then glazed.

"How long have you known Tony Rossi?"

"Six months."

"Good. You came from Chicago?"

"New York."

He was gone then, over the edge into pain-produced delirium. He cried, then babbled. One time he stopped, blinked at Mark and tried to point at him with his shattered arm. He cried again and stared at the Penetrator.

"Rossi family? Hell, we're on the move. Top drawer.

11

Real pros. Got the old man on ice, with a needle. That new kid, Tony, making every man jack of us jump. We're on the move, man!"

Then he tried to get up, but Mark held him. Primo's eyes narrowed, then glazed and he was blubbering again.

Primo suddenly felt light, weightless. He drifted through a garden of flowers and perfume. Quickly it changed and he was bumping over live coals that seared his flesh. His arms were being chewed off by crocodiles that swam at him out of the mists. Above, huge bats beat at him with black, webbed wings until he wanted to scream and bury himself in the white-hot coals below.

Mark smoothed the sand in front of Primo and waited for the delirium to ebb. A minute later he touched the man's cheek and he stirred, his eyes clearing.

"Hell, you wanna know about the Rossi family? Yeah, going like hell. More damn business than we can handle. Bringing in new men. Might start smuggling in aliens. High class, in a damn jet, important people. Charge them twenty, thirty thou for a ride."

"Where does Mrs. Tony Rossi live?"

"Moved her." He laughed, his voice winding up into a wild, hysterical cry. "Yeah, moved her to a good safe house, double security. She's so damn safe I never even been there."

"Why, Primo? Why is she so important?"

"Don't know."

Mark changed tactics. If Primo passed out again it

would take a doctor to revive him. "Look, old buddy. I got a little thing going with her, you know? Only I got to get there. She said to come up, but I don't know up where, get me?"

Primo snickered. "Hell, yes. Joke on old Tony. Right?"

"Where does she live?"

"Oh, up on Beeman Street, all the way to the lousy end of Beeman. On a damn cliff, up a canyon. Nobody gets in or out. Safe house." He closed his eyes and Mark let him fall sideways into the dry sand.

The big man watched the Mafia soldier for a few seconds, then nodded. He checked the tourniquet, making sure it held, then he put a small envelope into Primo's front pocket. It was a one-fix paper of heroin. He wanted this Mafia soldier to live to stand a rap for possession of horse. Mark looked at the Beretta. He shrugged and put the weapon back in his own belt. No sense wasting a good piece.

Ten minutes later Mark jogged the half mile to where he had parked his rented Pantera. He got in and drove toward a phone booth he had spotted earlier that night.

Mark Hardin was a large and powerful man. At six feet two, he was heavily muscled, with the lean, hungry look of an athlete in top condition. His complexion was dark and he suntanned to a coppery brown when he had the chance. He could move with the supple litheness of a cougar, and his dark eyes and thick black moustache gave his face, even in repose, a smoldering, critical look. When he frowned a cold, deadly aura seemed to hover over him.

Mark's hair was black and a little shaggy, hiding part of his ears and fighting with his collar. His usual weight was 205 pounds, which he maintained without conscious effort or diet. His accent, if any, was NBC news, but Easterners and those from the South soon picked up a slight far-West twang if they listened closely. The trouble was, many times Mark's enemies never had a chance to listen that long before they were dead.

Mark pushed open the door of the phone booth and left it ajar so the light wouldn't come on as he dialed a number.

"Boston Police Department," a voice answered.

"Narcotics squad, quick," he said.

The new voice came on almost at once, a man.

"Narcotics, Johnson."

"Hey, Narco, you better get yourself down to Carson Beach fast. A cat down there is selling horse like it's taffy. He's laid out on the sand now with a bullet hole in one arm and the other one broken. He's still got some heroin on him. I saw it. But you better get him quick or the damn tide is gonna drown him and take him out to sea."

Mark hung up before the detective could ask him any questions. He left the booth and got back in the sleek, dark maroon Pantera. As he drove he mulled over what Primo had said. The more he knew about this problem the less he understood it.

It began a little over a week ago. At first Mark didn't know whether to believe it or not. He had been in school with Tony Rossi at UCLA. Tony had been a fair halfback, but a brilliant tennis player, and had quit football in his sophomore year to spend all his time with tennis. He and Mark had double-dated, run around together a lot their senior year. Tony had been a sociology major and had more cash than he knew what to do with, a new car each year, and an apartment of his own.

It wasn't until his senior year at UCLA that Mark discovered Tony's old man was Carlo Rossi, Don Carlo, the Godfather of Boston, the Boston Family Mafioso.

But Tony hadn't followed in the Family footsteps. He hated the whole idea of where much of the money had come from in the old days, but swore now that the family was strictly legitimate. He was thinking about setting up a foundation in Los Angeles to help the poor.

Then the family situation blew. Tony and his old man had a wild argument during spring vacation, and Tony quit school, moved away from Boston, and got married. Next thing Mark knew Tony had signed on with a scientific expedition to go to Ghana and search for a lost tribe. He left his new wife at home expecting a child. Two years later Tony made news again. Mark heard about it when he was in 'Nam. Tony had signed for another expedition, this one to go to New Guinea to contact primitive headhunters who roam some of the islands. Almost at once the whole expedition vanished.

Only pieces of the boat were ever found and all members were declared missing.

Tony had shown up a year ago, unharmed, according to the news reports Mark had heard. Then the phone call came from Mark's old coach. It had been a roundabout message. Somebody wanted to see Mark in Boston. Someone who talked about certain double dates that only four people could know about, and the girls weren't going to talk about them. So it had to be Tony. But why all the secretiveness?

The person guessed that Mark's old coach would be able to find him, and had made the call. Two days later the coach called from Georgia, where he was working, and gave Mark the name of a small bar on Boston's east side where he should go, along with a date and a time.

The professor had encouraged Mark to go, take a breather after the Indian trouble at Taos. To see his old friend, relax, drop down to New York and see a few plays, maybe a performance of the New York City Ballet, or an opera. Get some culture. Mark was curious. Since Tony had lived through the expedition, he would have some hairy stories to tell. But why the cloak-and-dagger bit? Then Mark remembered that he wasn't the easiest person in the world to find.

So Mark had flown into Boston's Logan International Airport yesterday and made the meet. Just inside the door he stopped and fumbled at the cigarette machine without buying any and checked out the drinkers at the bar before he showed himself. Only one man was alone. He sat in a side booth without a drink.

16

Mark saw no hint of a weapon, and didn't recognize the man.

The face that turned toward Mark was thin, pale, cheeks too hollow, a nervous tic under one eye. His hair was a half-inch long, as if it were growing out from a shave job. A purple scar that had not healed properly slashed across his forehead. Mark guessed he was about six feet tall, then with a jolt he realized he knew this man. He would recognize those eyes anywhere, even as troubled as they were now.

"Tony?" the Penetrator asked in surprise. "What the hell happened to you?"

Tears surged up in the shadowy brown eyes and spilled down wan cheeks.

"Mark!" was all Tony could say as he grabbed Mark's hand with both of his. It was several seconds before he could say a word. At last he wiped away the moisture with his arm. Mark slid into the booth opposite him.

"Mark Hardin, right? UCLA. You played flanker back. I quit football for tennis. Remember?"

"Yeah, sure. I remember, Tony. What the hell . . . ?"

"UCLA. I had that apartment. Do you remember the Donovan twins, they were sophomores? Remember that night I had the pizza party? Remember what Sheryl did after she got a little high on the wine . . . ?"

Mark wanted to laugh, but he couldn't. The man who sat across from him was tortured, whipped, ready to give up. He looked as if he had been dragged through hell a million times but refused to quit, wouldn't die.

17

"Tony, I believe you, I know you're Tony Rossi, but what happened? You went to New Guinea, right? They found your ship all blown apart."

He nodded. His eyes darted to the door as it opened and Mark saw raw fear splash across his face, then vanish in a shiver that shook the frail body.

"Mark, I heard what you did in 'Nam, that big G.I. general you smashed."

"But, Tony! Didn't I read in the papers that about a year ago you escaped from some primitive tribe in New Guinea and got back home?"

"No, Mark, dammit, no! I didn't get away until a month ago. That bastard who says he's Tony Rossi, who's been living it up in my house and in the big place is a ringer, Mark. He's got my face and my car and my wife and my kid. *He's living in my skin!*"

Chapter Two

BANG, BANG, YOU'RE DEAD

Mark drove south on Interstate 95, got off at Hancock, and found Morrissey fronting on Quincy bay. He was trying to remember how to find the pad where he had driven Tony two days before.

After that first emotional reunion with Tony, Mark had bundled him into his car and taken him to a motel he had used before. That afternoon he took him to a doctor, who checked Tony over carefully. He was anemic, underweight, and in need of plenty of good food and sunshine. The doctor wasn't told where Tony had been the past four years. A day later Tony had moved out of the motel, saying he had to get away and think. He told Mark about a halfway house he had founded when he had been in town. It was a spot down on the beach run by and for street people. He said he could think the whole thing through down there.

From what Tony had told Mark in school, he had been the white sheep of the family. He sat back silently while his father was named Man of the Year, and won public service awards, and knew most of the good people of the Boston area, who discounted the slanderous rumors about Mafia connections.

Tony said he had funded a spot for beach people for three years, and thought he'd really helped some of them. He bought an old summer place, and sometimes on weekends would have fifteen kids sacked out there. Now he was going back to try to get his head together. Mark had been worried about the connection; now he knew why.

He parked as close to 21 Rover Lane as he could, locked the car, and walked down a long alley, then up another side alley until he could smell the salt spray in the air and hear a gull cry. He turned left under a Japanese *torii* gateway and saw the door ahead of him to number 21 Rover Lane standing open.

It was always open, to anyone. Mark stepped over a young girl lying in a sleeping bag just inside the entrance, then worked his way past three couples on the living room floor watching the movie on TV.

He knew where to find Tony. Upstairs there were two doors, one open, but Tony wasn't there. He didn't knock on the other door. No one ever knocked at 21 Rover Lane.

Mark opened the door to semi-darkness. One small candle flickered feebly in the far corner. Incense burned. A girl's voice came softly, lilting, singing some half-remembered, half-created lyric. It was a plaintive wail, an appeal.

As his eyes adjusted, he noticed a glint of metal and stopped moving. Mark stared at the muzzle of a big army .45 pistol. The thumb safety came off with a soft metallic *snic,* and Mark frowned.

"Peace, Tony, old buddy. Peace, it's Mark."

"Yeah, peace, freedom." It was Tony's voice but it was off key. "That's what the hell I'm looking for, right? Freedom away from these damn savages and their poison darts and mud houses."

Mark knew he was spaced out on fear and remembering. Tony hadn't touched anything since he'd been back. Not a drop of grape, not a whiff of Tijuana red, nothing with a needle or pills. He said that first day that Coca-Cola was the strongest thing his system could handle.

"Come on, Tony, don't give up. We'll get out of this damn place yet. They can't keep two good Italian boys penned up this way, not if we really work at it!"

Mark moved inside and shut the door when the .45 lowered. Tony was flashing back to his bad days in New Guinea. Very bad days. He hadn't really talked about them yet. Now Mark could make out the rest of the room. It was the same as the first time he had been there, only now a girl sat on a pillow. She had been singing; now she switched to a wooden flute.

"Tea, man? Want some of this bitchin' tea? The animals over here drink it all the time. Damn gooks!" Tony looked up suddenly, his eyes wide. "Hey, Mark, they get you too? Hell, thought maybe you got away."

"We got problems, old buddy, big problems."

Tony held up his hand. "Wait, get that slant-eyed bitch out of here," he said, pointing at the girl. "Says she don't speak English, but she probably knows it better than us. She's a damn spy for them sonsofbitches outside!"

The girl rose quickly. "He's been out of his head for hours. Can you keep him calmed down?"

Mark nodded and pointed to the door.

"Take care of him. He's a good one." She waved and left.

Mark took Tony's shoulders. "Tony, this is Mark. You're not in New Guinea any more. You're home, remember? Back in the States. We're both home now!"

Mark watched the man's face slowly change. First suspicion, then doubt, at last the idea took root and flourished. The smile that came was genuine.

"Home, yeah, Mark, home in the States." He scowled. "But dammit, not to my own house, my wife, my kid!"

Mark watched the man coming back from another world, from another time he didn't want to talk about. From captivity, threats, torture, from a primitive society where white men were either gods or devils, and both were delicacies on the tribal table. But when he escaped and came home he had discovered what real pain could be. Gradually his shoulders sagged and he looked at Mark. He was back now, all the way back from his retreat into fantasy, from his reliving of a time of pain to block out a newer, more threatening danger. He tried to face it.

22

"Mark, I just can't look it in the eye sometimes. Know what I mean? I have to haul-ass for a while." He shivered and took a deep breath.

"You talked to that guy I told you about?"

Mark nodded. "Yes, your wife and son are being held in a double-safe house. You couldn't get near it with a ten-man recon patrol. They have Monica and the kid and they'll keep them as insurance so they won't talk."

"And that bastard guy with my face is sleeping with Monica!"

"We don't know that, Tony. But don't blame her."

"Not her. I don't blame Monica at all. I know how they put it, how they talk things over, how they reason with you, until you have only one way to go—do it their way or die. Dammit, I know! I was teethed on it. Some kids don't realize what their dads do as they grow up. Hell, I knew from the time I was in the second grade. I understand these people, Mark. I know how they think, how they react. That's why I wouldn't go into the Family business."

Mark grunted and shifted positions on the pillow. "That's another reason you have to get out of this pad," he said. "They'll hear this place is open again, and some soldiers will come past to see why. If they find you here . . ."

Tony snorted. "I'll take seven of them with me," he said, waving the .45. Then he shook his head. "Yeah, you're right. They must have a standing contract on me with everybody who knows the score. Wonder what my dead body is worth?"

He stood and padded around the room barefooted. "It's got to be the way you laid it out that first night. Dad must have been losing his grip, getting too old to think on his feet. Maybe he got sick, I don't know, but somebody moved in on him. They couldn't just blast half the boys and take over, not with his reputation here in town. So they do it cute. I'd been missing for what, two years? So they say, what the hell, the kid's been zapped. All we have to do is find some joker about the same size and coloring who looks something like Tony, then get a makeup man to do the rest. Maybe throw on a moustache or beard and say Tony's changed a lot since he escaped from the primitives."

"Somebody did a damn good job for them, Tony. I saw that joker one night on nationwide TV—after he got "home." I tried to telephone you but you were *out*. Damn, I was sure it was you."

"Yeah, they set it up solid, and with all the contacts Dad had in this town it would be a snap. First thing they would do would be exchange my police fingerprint card for the new man's. The police work on other positive I.D., too, like medical and dental X-rays and records. Dad's had his own doctors for years, so pumping in fake charts, prints, and X-rays would be a snap."

"Tony, just who is the power behind this ringer? Doesn't it have to be one of your dad's top lieutenants?"

"Yeah. I've tried to come up with a name for three days now. It could be three or four guys I knew before, but in those three years I've been gone, I don't know

24

what happened. Might be somebody entirely new who just moved in and took over."

"And as far as the rest of the Mafia, *la commizzioni* that controls all the Families, knows, the real Tony came back and took over for his ailing father?"

"Right, business as usual." Tony sat down again, letting out a pent-up breath. "Can you imagine the control they must have over that guy? They must have him trussed up like a puppet. He says what they tell him to; if he goofs in public, they cover for him. They countermand any wrong orders he gives and keep him under lock and key so tight he must be talking in falsetto by now. Almost a year he's been doing it, right?"

Mark nodded. "But now it's your ball game, Tony. You get to call some shots for a change. I'll help you where I can, like getting your wife back."

"I wouldn't ask you to help me take over the Family. I don't want that. I want my wife and kid back and to get Dad free. But if it means blowing apart the Rossi family rackets to do it, we'll do it! We'll blast the Rossi Mafia organization to hell."

Mark watched him. At least the aborigines hadn't bled the fight and the guts out of Tony. He was still one tough Italian.

"First, buddy, we get you out of this pad, right now. When the Family finds Primo, they're going to get curious in a big rush."

A flicker of interest showed in Tony's eyes. "You have to mess him up a little before he cooperated?"

Mark told him, and Tony laughed scornfully. "Yeah, champ, you're still one mean sonofabitch." Tony

25

jumped up, kicked a pillow, then snapped a wall switch, flooding the room with light. They both squinted.

"I'll be packed in five minutes. Just my straw bag and my trusty .45." He hefted the weapon. "That's the first damn thing I bought when I hit town; crazy, huh?" He shrugged. "That offer to use part of your pad still open?"

Ten minutes later they left; Tony told Mark the people staying there would run the halfway house. As they drove back toward town, Mark looked over at Tony.

"How are you fixed for bread? I never thought about that before."

"Who needs it?"

"You do. Now that you're not with the people. And you can't get any that belongs to you in those banks, right?"

Tony scowled, pushed lower in the Pantera seat.

Mark let it cook for two blocks, then turned off the boulevard, angling for the downtown section. He found the street he wanted and cruised along up the hill, then turned right and parked. They were half a block off Dorchester, one empty lot from an alley. Mark pulled his Colt Commander .45 from his belt and checked the clip. It had seven rounds.

"Tony, I figure it's time the Family returned a little of the interest they've been spending on your share of the business. For openers, I suggest a little visit with DiMatteo. Remember him?"

Tony shook his head.

"DiMatteo runs the biggest collection bank in this end of town, for the Rossi family. Oh, yes, Tony, I know about policy games going here now, the old numbers game, and the bookmaking is worth a real bundle these days too. Unless the schedule's been changed, this is about the right time of night for the regular collection. What you need is a stake, Tony, some cash to tide you over until we get your wife and family out of there."

Tony was starting to grin. "Just like that, we bust some heads, only this time we take the coin, right?"

"Right. We relieve DiMatteo of some of his long green, and he isn't about to yell robbery. Actually what we're doing is redistributing some of the wealth."

Tony dug into his straw case and came out with the .45. "Loaded and locked," he said. "Seven rounds in the clip, one in the chamber."

Mark gave him a thumbs-up sign and sat there, judging the odds. None of the counters or bag men would know him or Tony. DiMatteo himself wouldn't be in until the take for the day had been counted. There might be four men, two counting, two soldiers, maybe a driver. A piece of cake.

They left the car and walked quietly into the alley. It was a business district on one side, and apartments on the other. The alley was walled with gates. Mark picked the right one and went through it after a slow and careful recon of the small back parking lot. It was clean.

Mark ran silently to the rear door, with Tony right

27

behind him. They would make a fast hit and then vanish. The rear door was locked. Mark laughed at the lock. A plastic credit card was all he needed to open the door.

A few seconds later they were inside a hallway with two doors halfway down. Mark listened at one, moved to the next, and nodded. He turned the knob gently with his left hand, then kicked the door open, his right fist full of his .45 Commander.

Three men sitting around a square table looked up in surprise. On the table were stacks of bills held with rubber bands.

"Freeze!" Mark shouted at the men. "Hands stay right on the table. Don't push any damn buzzers or you're all three dead men. Got that?"

One of the three broke into a sweat, his hands shaking uncontrollably. He trembled so hard Mark thought he might fall off his chair. Mark leaped to the table, pulled the frightened man from his chair, and threw him against the wall, where he crumpled, sliding down it like a straw doll.

"Hands on your heads, both of you. Lace your fingers. Do it *now*!"

The two men did as they were told. Tony stood in the doorway, his big .45 covering the men. One of the men stared at Tony.

"Face the wall, stupid!" Mark snapped. Already he had spotted the container he would use, a newspaper boy's paper bag for his bike. Mark grabbed it and began sweeping the stacks of fives, tens, and twenties into the bag. He saw a small stack of fifties and hundreds and pushed them in too, topping off the bag with stacks of ones.

During the operation Mark had to lower his gun, and as he worked he saw one of the men begin to move his hand. Then he bent and spun around. Mark fired his .45; the booming roar in the small, closed room crashed deafeningly. Then Tony's .45 blasted and the second man spun to the side, slamming against the wall. Mark jumped to the injured men and picked up the weapons they had dropped. Mark's man had a bullet in his throat, splattering blood on the wall and floor. The other Mafia soldier had caught the big slug in his left side, smashing him to the wall. Mark waved at Tony to check the hall.

Tony looked out carefully, saw no one, and signaled that it was clear.

Mark caught up the newspaper bag full of money and they ran down the hall toward the back door. A man bolted from the second room in front of them. Mark crashed into him with a head-high shoulder block, blasting the man against the wall as he and Tony stormed past and out the back door. They sprinted for the back gate, ran down the alley, and up the street to the Pantera. Inside the car, Mark took three deep breaths, then started the machine and eased away from the curb. He drove at fifteen miles an hour as he turned in front of the little grocery store they had so recently attacked through the back door. There were no lights showing in the front windows. Mark laughed softly and grinned at Tony.

"One home run for our team. If I'd known this was so easy, I'd have tried it sooner. Now at least you have some operating capital." Mark growled. "You touch anything inside?"

"Just my .45."

"Good; the Family could put a fingerprint man in there, and I want to be sure we're clean."

"You do this often, Mark?" Tony asked.

"Now and then."

Tony sat up straighter and fastened his seat belt; then he turned on the radio and found soft music.

"You know, that's what I missed most, the music, a radio, some TV or a stereo. That was rough to do without." He blinked and eyed Mark. "Okay, star. Say you are right about what went on in the Family. That means they have to maintain Monica and little Tony for occasional public appearances with the man in my skin, right? So it all looks normal. We just hit them for a few thousand, but what can we do *now or ever* about getting Monica and the boy away from them?"

"We work at it, Tony. I recon the place, we get all the G-2 we can on it, and then we plan it out so it can't miss. I know that rescue mission is at the top of your list. But we can't afford to risk messing this one, right?"

Tony sighed. "With all the emphasis on family, they've got to maintain her. Otherwise somebody would start to get suspicious. Used to be Mafia men were fair game, no season. But no Family man worth his medallion would lift one little Italian pinkie against

30

wife or kin of a Cosa Nostra member. Times do change."

"Michael Sollozzo, know him?"

"Sure. He was a top man with Dad, had been for years. Dad said he trusted him like a son."

"He shouldn't have. Primo said Michael has taken over and they have your father on some kind of drugs."

"For a year? That could kill him!"

"We'll get him out too, Tony. Now what do you remember about Sollozzo?"

Tony stared out the window at a row of trees bordering the street. "Efficient. He was a hit man for a while in New York until the cops hassled him out of town. Dad used him a lot as a supervisor. He did almost everything for Dad as an assistant. He must have known every detail of the operations so he could move in without a hitch."

"And he's a killer?"

"I don't like to use that . . ." Tony stopped. He rubbed his face with both hands. "I guess there are going to be a lot of things I'll have to face up to, and remember. Yes, Mike Sollozzo is a killer: cold, ruthless, nerveless, absolutely amoral."

"So we attack them, right up the gut. You say you know how they think. What would their response be if we wiped out the man in your skin? If we laid off and brought him down with a .300 Weatherby magnum? If the king is dead, does his family go free?"

"Not a chance, Mark. They know too much. Sollozzo would never let them out that way. Monica won't get free unless we go in and blast her out. Whatever promises they made to her were lies."

"Then an all-out assault on the safe house wouldn't work either. If we did gun our way inside it would be too late."

"Yes. Sollozzo will take no chances. The guards there must have instructions about prisoners. If anybody tries to break in or gets the upper hand, my family gets zapped fast."

"Which means we settle down, take it easy, go slow and carefully. We make sure of every move. We hit how and where we can, making sure not to endanger Monica or the boy."

Tony nodded. "It has to be neat and positive and quick. Once they get the idea somebody is moving in, they'll tighten up the whole operation like a turtle in his shell. And if they get the hint that I'm alive and back in town, Monica won't last ten minutes. I've come back too far from the damned natives to lose the fight now. I want my family back!"

· A half hour later Mark pulled the rented Pantera into the motel parking lot, backing into the slot.

They walked to the outside motel room and went in.

"We'll get your family out, Tony. Don't worry about it. I've become something of a specialist in this kind of project."

Tony waved and went into the bathroom. Mark had just started to take his coat off when a knock sounded on the door. He checked his watch, saw that it was after midnight, and shrugged.

He opened the door and looked down at a dark-eyed girl in an expensive dress with a plunging neckline and a mink around her pretty shoulders.

She smiled. "Are you Mr. Hardin? Mark Hardin?"

Mark frowned but nodded. Nobody but the professor knew he was here.

"May I come in for a moment? I have a message for you."

He stepped back, let her come inside, and closed the door. He stared at the expensive diamond necklace on her tanned chest. She stood model-like for a moment, with her hands behind her, hips turned to de-emphasize them. But her smile was strained.

"Now what was the message?" Mark asked.

"This!" She pulled a gun from behind her back and, holding it with both hands, aimed at him and fired.

Chapter Three

THIRD-STORY VISIT

Mark Hardin's eyes darted to the girl's face, and he evaluated her determination in that fraction of a second before the gun went off. By the time her finger tightened on the trigger he was watching it, estimating the amount of trigger pull necessary. Before her finger had moved what he guessed was half of the trigger distance, he let out an army bayonet practice field yell and at the same time dove almost directly toward her, but just enough to one side so he could watch her movement.

The Penetrator hit the carpet with his shoulder, rolling at once toward the pair of pretty legs. He heard the weapon go off over his head and knew she hadn't had time to let up on the trigger or change her aim; then he crashed into her, jolting her backwards, sprawling her on the floor, ripping her skirt to the waist, exposing perfect legs and the top of her pantyhose.

Mark heard her handbag hit the floor somewhere behind him as he rolled again, coming full length on top of her. He grabbed for her flailing hands and felt her trim body twisting under him, saw her free hand come at his face, trying to scratch. She didn't make a sound. He had the gun hand pinned against the floor when he heard movement at the bathroom doorway behind him.

"What the hell?"

Mark pulled the gun from her hand and slid it across the floor toward Tony, then pressed her hands against the carpet. He leaned up and looked at her. The expensive dress had a rip in it now, exposing one tanned, braless breast.

The girl glared at Mark, then looked toward the door.

"Tony?" she wailed. "Tony, is that really you?"

He walked toward them, curious, then his expression changed. "Angie!" he cried. He rushed to them. "Angie, you tried to shoot Mark?" He shook his head. "Old buddy, you can let this vicious mad-dog killer get up. She's harmless. First the introductions. Mark, I'd like to present my sister, Angie Rossi. Angie, meet Mark."

Mark was stunned. "Your sister . . . ?"

He let go of her hands and stood. "Your sister? You didn't tell me that you had a . . ." He snorted and nodded. "Oh, damn . . . sure. Angie Rossi. Seven years ago you were in the society columns almost every day."

He stared at her, then reached for her hand to help her up. "You've . . . ah, changed."

She ignored him, shrugging back into her dress.

"Tony, is that you?" She sat up. "So pale, thin, and your hair, so short." She paused, eyes narrowing. "It is you, Tony! I know it's you." She jumped up and ran to him. "I still don't understand it. You came home a year ago, but you didn't answer my calls, then suddenly I get your message and I'm confused. Why all the secrecy?"

She put her arms around him. "I didn't know what to think when you phoned. We've got a million things to talk about. And you need some pasta to fatten you up."

Tony was crying and laughing at once.

"Same old Angie, mile a minute. Supermouth, I called you. We'll explain it all later. Now say hello to Mark, my good friend from UCLA."

She sighed and glanced at Mark, then looked away. A wry smile touched her lovely features. "What can I say to a man I just tried to kill? I mean, do I say I'm glad I'm a lousy shot, or just 'How do you do,' in my old European cultured accent? That would be stupid." She smiled. "I'm really sorry I tried to blow off your head." She dropped to a couch, suddenly contrite. "I'm so ashamed!" A gush of tears came down her cheeks. "I thought Tony said somebody had taken over the Family and was holding Daddy and Monica and little Tony, and he said something about Mark and so I came to the number Tony gave me when I got here. I bought this dumb little gun . . ."

Tony watched her, shook his head in amused disbelief. He sat beside her and patted away the tears. "Angie, you're partly right. They put a ringer in for me and somebody did take over our house and the Family businesses. But Mark isn't the one. He's trying to—"

"—trying to help us." She finished it for him. "Now I remember. I was so furious and so tired, and just plain mad. I didn't get it right, and with almost twenty-four hours on planes and waiting for planes, and arguing about tickets and trying to watch my baggage, and be sure it got on the right planes . . ."

Mark watched her. Tired and ripped, crying and embarrassed, she was still dazzling, remarkably beautiful, and now, contrite, she became so appealing he wanted to pick her up and cuddle her.

"Sorry I was so rough. If I'd known . . ."

She turned and looked at him with sharp brown eyes.

"No, Mark, you were easy on me. You should have slugged me right in my big mouth. Glad I'm a damn poor shot. I swore I'd never use one of those things." She paused and looked at Tony.

"Poor Tony. Captured and escaped and now somebody is taking your place. Darling, we're going to get it all fixed. It's going to be just fine. Mark will help us. You should have seen the way he took that gun away from me." She glanced up at Mark, then put her arms around Tony again.

"Darling, we've been apart so long. Remember I went to take my last two years of college in Switzerland, then decided to stay for a year in Paris. I went to

Rome for a year and the time just evaporated." She looked over Tony's shoulder at the Penetrator. "Now, Mark is going to help us; I know he will. He was your friend in school, right?"

Mark jumped into the void when she took a breath. "Why don't we all relax and you two can have your reunion."

They agreed and Angie gasped.

"Tony, it's been almost three years since you've seen little Tony."

Tony's forced smile shaded into a frown. "True." In the one word he loaded anger, impatience, and frustration.

"But how did you get this address?" Mark asked, always worried about his own security.

"Oh, Tony gave it to me when he phoned me in Rome. I don't know how he ever found me. If I hadn't left my number with my best friend Mitzi . . ."

She touched his arm and Mark turned. "I'm so ashamed about that dumb trick with the gun. I could have hurt you. All this women's lib thing and then I go and do a stupid, typically idiotic-female thing like that."

"Forget it; you missed. All is forgiven."

Her eyes held his for a moment, and he thought he saw them soften a little.

She relaxed on the white and gold sofa, pushing the torn part of her dress back in place. It didn't seem to worry her.

"Now for our reunion. Tony, tell me just everything that happened. How you got away, how you got home, all of it." She curled her shoeless feet under her hips. "We've got the rest of the night and all day tomorrow."

They talked for three hours straight, with Mark in the background. They had five years to catch up on.

It was five A.M. when Angie began to walk around the little bedroom, scowling. "Now that the small talk is over, let's get down to business. How in hell are we going to stand up to Michael Sollozzo and the whole Rossi power structure? And how can we get Monica and Dad away from them?"

Tony looked at Mark. "Big gunner?"

"Angie, how much do you know about your father's business here?"

"Relax, Mark. I've known since before high school that Dad was the Boston Mafia. I knew some of his dealings were illegal and crooked, and I simply pushed it out of my mind and ignored the whole thing. Now I can't ignore it. So he's a Mafia Don; he's still my father, and I love him and I want to help him."

The small muscle at the corner of Mark's mouth twitched. This was a hell of a smart girl. He wouldn't have to worry about her.

"Good; I appreciate knowing that. Now the way I see it, first we go for the hostages, Monica and little Tony and your father. Just how we do it, and when, is going to take a lot of planning."

"The first thing we should do is get word to Monica," Angie said. "Let her know her husband is really alive and well and working to get her free. The poor girl must be living in constant terror. We don't want her doing anything to hurt her chances of coming out of this."

Tony agreed. He blinked. "That should be enough to work on for now. I'm beat, you guys. Anybody mind if I just sack out?"

"Hey, it's almost six A.M.," Angie said. "I think I'll get back to the hotel. I'll take a cab."

"Stay here if you want to," Mark offered.

She smiled, a devilish grin threatening to take over her whole face. "Thanks, Mark; I could, but all of my things are at the hotel."

She took a cab a few minutes later.

Mark got up at noon that Wednesday, had breakfast, and made two phone calls. Then he took a pair of 8-power binoculars and, after spending half an hour with a set of maps, drove toward Beeman Street, with its nearby maze of dead-end roads, curved avenues, and one-way splits.

He assumed the Beeman Street entrance would be guarded, probably with steel gates, watchmen, and dogs. What interested him more was the back door, looking out over the small cliff on which the house perched.

He drove to within a block of the canyon from the other side, stopped the car, and picked up his binoculars. Then he walked down a side street to the edge of the canyon. He angled into the high weeds and worked down to a grove of tall trees. The canyon had a gentle slope on this side. From behind a young, leafy tree he studied the cliff opposite him. It was eighty feet high, made of hard sandstone that had stratified and was crumbling. The top had no fence, only a shield of shrubs which cut off any view of the house, except for the roof of what he guessed was the third story. He studied the face of the rock wall again. It developed a slight overhang near the top. That fact, plus the softness of the layered sandstone, would make it a hard climb.

There was no doubt about it being the right house. It was the only one that was perched on the dropoff at the head of the canyon.

There seemed to be no protection devices aimed into the canyon. Evidently they considered that position safe. Mark checked out the terrain from his present location to the base of the cliff. He wanted to memorize it in the daylight so he could get across it more easily in the dark. There was plenty of tall grass and scrub brush for concealment. A few clumps of heavy brush grew near the base of the cliff.

The Penetrator put the binoculars under his shirt and walked to the car. He's seen enough.

Back at the midtown motel he assembled his gear and double-checked it. Tony watched.

"What's my assignment tonight?" Tony asked. He had been on the phone for two hours with Angie, talking about the good old days. She wanted to get together for another talk that night, but Tony told her about the visit they had planned to the safe house.

"Your job is driver, commo man, and backup," Mark said. He coiled the quarter-inch nylon rope and tied the end with a never-slip knot to an eight-pronged, any-angle grappling hook.

"I'll have a transmission-only radio set in my pocket. If I get into trouble, I'll beep it twice. That means get your ass over there to the cliff on the double."

"That's all? I want to go in with you and see Monica!"

"No way. It'll be risky enough with one body getting into that stronghold. Two would be sure disaster. We agreed to get word to your wife, but that's my job. If it's possible I want to get in and out without them knowing about it. That way we don't tip them off that anything is wrong."

"They must smell a rat already. Before you came back I took that rented LTD and drove over to the beach. I sneaked up where I could see Twenty-One. Not a kid around it, but the door was open. After a while a big guy came outside and threw away a smoke. He was a Mafia soldier. Some of the kids must have talked."

Mark hooded his eyes with thick black brows.

"But all they've got is a worry," Mark said. "Could have been anybody opened up Twenty-One. Anyway, that's one more reason to keep you away from that safe house."

They left the motel at 10:15, just after checking with Angie. The low fog bank had swirled in, swallowing Boston in one huge gulp. Mark hoped the fog would help him. For an hour they waited, watching the scene from Tony's rented LTD, parked near the end of the side street.

At 11:30 Mark put on dark blue coveralls and stuffed the borrowed Beretta, with a full clip, into one of the big pockets. The weapon was locked and loaded with one round in the chamber, a total of nine shots.

"Tony, I may have to prove to Monica that you're the real Tony, and that you're back. How can I convince her?"

Tony thought for a moment. "Tell her about our wedding night. No one else knows what happened. It was wild. We never got to the honeymoon hotel, spent the whole night parked in the woods. Somebody sabotaged our car, mixed up the spark plug wires, so we had almost no power."

Mark nodded and reached into one of his pockets; he pushed a button twice. Two low beeps sounded over the small receiver on the dash.

"That's the trouble call. But I don't expect any. I plan on getting to the top of the cliff just a little before midnight. They should be settled down in the house by then."

He left.

The route through the canyon proved to be as quick and easy as he had figured it would. At the cliff he brushed aside the growth and checked the rock. Crumbling. That would make it more dangerous to climb. With the overhang there was no way he could climb it without the rope.

As he uncoiled the thin nylon line, the fog bank moved over the cliff like a huge, foraging gastropod. He recoiled the rope, testing the knots, and checked the eight-pronged hook again. It was only eight inches across and made of aluminum. He twirled it twice on three feet of line to get the feel. Then he swung it once more and threw it upward. It hit the face of the rocks and rattled to the bottom. He remained motionless, waiting for any reaction. He heard nothing. Mark walked to the hook, recoiling the rope in bigger loops to cut down the drag of the playing-out line.

On the third throw the hook went over the top and caught. It snagged on something when he started to pull. As it firmed, he put his whole weight on the line until the hook would move no more. He grunted and began to move up the line, hand over hand, his feet scrambling up the cliff. He wore thin leather gloves to protect his hands.

Escape and evasion training in the army had started his interest in rope work, and for two years he had taken lessons in hard-rock climbing. Now he moved upward steadily, using footholds where he could find them. The overhang wasn't as pronounced as he had at first thought. By pivoting to the left he could go around most of it. Mark kept working upward.

As his eyes came up level with the lip of the cliff he paused, found firm rests for his feet, and checked the grounds. The hook had caught directly behind the three-inch trunk of a flowering shrub. He saw no movement on the fifty feet of lawn ahead of him. Spotlights shone on the yard, played along each of the walls, and bathed the sides of the house.

The fog rolled in heavier now, in gray, wet waves. Mark bellied over the top edge of the cliff and relaxed on the cool of the grass. He waited. There was no rush.

Sooner or later someone would move or show himself if there were back yard guards. He didn't expect anyone here. The Penetrator scoured the area for any cigarette glow, any out-of-place shape, any movement. He could spot no evidence of a guard.

Without warning, the yard lights snapped off. Mark closed his eyes, then tried to read the luminous dial on his watch. Midnight. Evidently they thought the back so naturally protected they doused the security lights at midnight. That would mean no Mafia soldier guards back here either. He gave himself three more minutes to get his eyes accustomed to the blackness, then moved ahead through the shrubs, walking carefully, checking each step as he would in an enemy mine field. At the edge of the plant line he found a trip wire. It was tensioned for activation by pressure from either side, top or bottom.

Mark stepped over it, checked for a second surprise wire, found none, and moved onto the edge of the grass toward a stack of firewood near the side fence. It bordered a first-floor roof. He crawled onto the first-floor roof from the fence and stopped. He guessed the captive family would be on the third floor. It would be the easiest place to contain them.

The Penetrator climbed to the second floor on a hip roof and paused, listening for any activity below. He wore crepe-soled shoes that were noiseless on the asphalt shingles. Mark looked in one window. It seemed to be an unoccupied room. He spotted an old drainpipe going up to the third floor and tested it critically, decided it would hold his weight, and went up it, stepping on the joints and climbing carefully. It was a delicate maneuver. At the window he took out a small pencil flash and shone it through the glass. The room held one bed, and a small boy was sprawled on it. Mark cut the light and tried the window. It was old-fashioned, wooden-framed and sash weighted, and the first time he tried the window moved upward with a soft squeak. He powered it as high as it would go and wiggled through into the room. Mark left the boy undisturbed, closed the window, and tested the door. It was unlocked and opened onto a hallway, down which he saw the soft bluish glow of a TV picture tube. The sound came muted.

He saw two more doors opening off the hallway and a stairway extending down into darkness. Mark headed silently toward the TV picture glow. Edging up to the door frame, he peered around and saw a young woman sitting in a chair brushing her long hair. She wore a thin, pink nightie and slippers. Johnny Carson cracked jokes on the Tonight Show, but Monica Rossi wasn't laughing. She was just as Tony had described her, right down to the small mole near her nose.

He could see no one else in the room, so he decided a quick move would be best. He coughed and stepped into the room.

"Monica, I'm a friend; please don't make a sound." His voice was soft, gentle.

She snapped her head back, her wide, frightened eyes staring at him. One hand came to her mouth, the other dropped the hairbrush. She sat perfectly still, not trying to cover herself, too startled to scream.

She was a large woman, with solid shoulders, a firm neck, and expressive brown eyes. Her thin-lipped mouth and straight nose gave her the classic Italian profile, and it all came together into an attractive, appealing face.

"Don't be frightened, Monica. I'm a friend. I've been talking with Angie, Angie Rossi. She's back in town but the Family doesn't know about it. She wants to help you get out of here. I just broke in, and they don't know I'm here. Are you all right?"

She nodded, turned to reach for her robe. Long habit forced her to turn back.

"May I put on my robe?"

"Of course. Angie knows you're being held a prisoner here with little Tony. We're trying to help. Are you ready for a surprise?"

"I've had my share lately." Her brown eyes confronted him. "It would be nice if it could be good news for a change."

"Monica, I know the man who says he's your husband is not. He's an actor, a substitute."

Her hands came to her mouth to cover a gasp. "Don't say that. They'll kill us all, they told me . . ."

"Monica. The reason I know this is because the real Tony Rossi is staying in my motel. He isn't dead; he did get captured but he escaped two months ago."

He waited for a reaction. None came. Finally she sighed.

"Is he another imposter?"

He told her then what Tony had said about their wedding night, including some intimate details about

48

how they made love on the back seat of the car, afraid they would be discovered.

When he finished she was sobbing quietly into a handkerchief. "I was in school with Tony, Monica. When he got to the States he called me. Physically he's in good shape, and he misses you. He says he'll get you out of here as soon as he can. But be sure you don't let on that you know the real Tony is back."

She wiped at her eyes, but now they held a new glint of purpose. "I know. I understand." Her face tried to smile. "It seems too good to be true. Tony is really back!"

"He wanted to be sure you don't do anything that would put you or little Tony in danger. We'll work at it as fast as we can, but it might take a week or so."

She laughed softly. "A week we can do standing on our heads." She moved over and kissed his cheek. "Thank you. I don't even know your name, or why you're doing this, but be careful. Those men downstairs will kill you if they find you on the grounds."

They had been talking in whispers as the TV set droned on.

"Are you going out in public soon, to a meeting or a party?"

"I don't think so. The last time we went out little Tony started to cry and said he didn't want to come home. It caused a big problem and they thought we were trying to escape. No, we won't be going out again soon."

"It shouldn't be more than a week. We don't know

49

how or when, but remember, Tony's back, and he has only one purpose in life, to get you and his son out of here. I'd better split."

She went with him to the window of the boy's room.

"At night they have three guards. Be careful."

He nodded, went out the window and silently down the heavy drainpipe. He heard the window close softly above him. Mark worked his way quietly over the roof, well aware how footsteps on an overhead can be heard below. He got down to the fence and was about to jump to the ground when a flashlight beam snapped on, catching him in the face.

"Hold it!" a voice snarled. A gun went off as Mark jumped off the fence, rolling when he hit the grass. He jerked out the Beretta, looking for the light. It swung toward him and Mark snapped a shot to the right of the beam. The light fell to the ground and he heard a groan. Mark ran for the cliff, stepped over the wire, and had just vanished down the edge of the dropoff on the rope when the back-yard lights came on.

Mark still wore the tough leather gloves, but he hadn't taken time to put the rope around him so he could rappell down. He corrected himself as he slid down the rope. No, rappelling was a two-rope system with a *D* ring. He slid until he thought the rope would burn his hands off, stopped and went hand over hand, then slid again. He heard voices above him. At least the overhang kept them from looking directly down at him.

But they would see the nylon line. He tried to slide

again, but the leather gloves were on fire. He heard a snarl from above and felt his slim support vibrate. A split second later the line he held gave way and he was falling.

Chapter Four

WAITING TO DIE

Mark dropped the rope and tried to turn so he could land on his feet. His shoulder smashed into and past an outcropping of sandstone; then he turned, not able to stop. Without a warning he crashed into the brush at the foot of the cliff. It was the same growth he had fought with when he went up the cliff a few minutes before. Now it saved him.

The heavy brush bent double with his weight, snapping some branches, breaking his fall. He hit hard on his side, rolled over, and winced as he felt the pain in his back.

Not the damn back, not now, he told himself as he tried to get to his feet. His head ached; his back throbbed with the old grinding pain, and he tried to stand. Ahead he saw only a blur of shapes and forms.

Mark shook his head from side to side, closing his

53

eyes, hoping things would come into focus when he opened them. One eye cleared and he stood, tried to find the same path he had used to come in. He couldn't. He ran toward the street, crashing through small brush and weeds. Once he missed his footing in a rain-eroded gully and fell. He hit the ground hard but rolled and was up again. This time both his eyes were clear. He ran, plotting the Mafioso's next moves. They would recon, try to get a car around here as soon as possible, hoping to find his body. Maybe they would lower someone over the cliff? No, it would be the car. He had to move!

The Penetrator ran faster, floundered into a tree, backed off, and in one more burst came into the street. He had his balance back by the time he pounded up the half block of blacktop and slid into the car.

The first thing he saw was Tony's black .45 automatic muzzle six inches from his face.

"Easy, Tony, and get the hell out of here. I made contact. We'll have company in a few seconds."

"Yeah, I heard your cap pistol," Tony said, gunning the LTD. The wheels spun as it jolted away from the curb and tore down the street. The LTD was a block beyond the intersection turning left when a big Caddy crew wagon squealed around the corner and roared into the narrow side street they had just left.

"Mark . . . Monica?"

"She's fine, Tony. Monica and little Tony are both in great shape. They're on the top floor of the place; nobody is up there with them. Lots of muscle down below, though. I told her about you, that you're really alive and here and mad as hell."

"Is her hair still long? She didn't cut it, did she?"

Mark smiled at the reaction, but shook his head. "No, I don't think so, Tony. It comes halfway to her waist. She's holding up beautifully. Says she can stand on her head for a week if she has to."

"A week?" Tony asked, his face clouding.

"We need some time, Tony. We have to do this right. We have to probe and find some weak spots, get some leverage. It takes time to move in on an entrenched enemy like this one."

"I can tell you all about the Big Place, the Family mansion where we used to live. I've never been to the house where they have Monica."

"Good, Tony, I'll need that info about the mansion. Now get back to the damn motel, will you? I'm a little rocky."

"You hurt, get hit?"

"Just some hurt pride. They chopped my rope and I fell. Nothing broken."

"Get you right there." Tony jammed down on the gas.

"Easy, Tony. We don't want a speeding ticket. Keep it down and legal. Some traffic cop might wonder why I've got all these deadly little toys and why you have that big .45 without a permit."

Fifteen minutes later they had parked the LTD and put away the special suitcase of equipment from the trunk. Mark had cleaned his .45 and checked his bag of sudden death. He had explosives, timers, ammunition, even a folding stock rifle in case he needed a long-range weapon. He had dropped the Beretta when the rope gave way. At least he wouldn't have to clean it.

As Tony assembled his .45 he began mumbling and nodding to himself. He stopped suddenly.

"Sorry, I used to talk to myself all the time over there. I wanted to hear some voice I could understand. Just now I was trying to put something together. Dad used to take care of some old lady, one of our aunts, I think. They had her in a dozen homes, and finally Dad just bought a place and told them to keep her."

Tony finished with the .45, pulled back the slide, then let the hammer down carefully.

"Yeah, it was called the Cloisters Rest Home. Suppose that's where they've stashed Dad? The Family owns the place."

"It's worth a try, but don't you go there. Somebody would recognize you and our whole play would be blown." Mark stared at Tony. "In fact, why don't you grow a beard?"

"A beard? I just got rid of the one from New Guinea."

"Grow it again, a full one. It might save your hide in case somebody sees you who shouldn't."

The next morning Mark left Tony at the motel and drove to the Cloisters Rest Home. The Penetrator wore plain brown pants and a sports shirt. In one hand he carried a potted plant and in the other a white envelope with the name of Mrs. Lola Smith on it. It was a little past ten A.M. when he pushed through the front door and walked confidently past a nurse's station and information desk and into a long corridor. The place was for real. Three nurses walked past him, one with a tray of drugs.

He heard a plaintive cry from some elderly woman: "Help! Help! Help!" A moment later the calls for help came again. No one paid any attention to them. An aide, a janitor, and two nurses ignored the calls.

He moved on down the hall and looked in the first open door. A white-haired man, wasted away to a hundred pounds, lay on his slanted hospital bed. On the front of his hospital gown was a large, blood-red splotch. His sad, slow-moving eyes stared at the ceiling; his mouth was open as he sucked air into his protesting lungs in a whistling wheeze.

Through the next door he saw an old woman, shrunken and wasted, sitting in a wheelchair looking down the corridor. She tried to talk to everyone who passed, but couldn't lift her head from one shoulder where it lay. Her voice came garbled and broken and few could understand her. Light blue eyes gave the only color to her face. One nurse listened to her.

"Oh, you want to get back in bed. Fine, dear. Just a minute and I'll help you."

"No," the old woman said distinctly, but the nurse wheeled her back into her room, not listening.

All the way down the twenty-room hallway scenes repeated; only the faces changed. The bodies found new and angry ways to torment the souls, bodies with eyes mirroring the suffering of lost hope, creating a scrap heap of human beings waiting, wishing for death.

Mark walked to the end of the corridor, turned left, and found more rooms and patients. He wasn't sure what he expected, but he knew what he was hunting: locked doors, areas of limited or no access.

The cross hallway opened to the left again, taking him back in the direction he had come. The nursing home was on one floor, laid out in a giant square. Nowhere were there any locked doors. The medical personnel looked efficient, friendly, over-worked, and, he was sure, half-dulled to human suffering. In the last room he found an old woman with a patch over one eye and a tube up her nose and probably down her throat, to be used for eating. Her lips were swollen, red-splotched.

Her black eyes caught his attention, and he put the potted plant down on her night stand, smiled, pocketed the fake card, and hurried out the front door of the nursing home.

He'd give odds of a thousand to one that Don Carlo Rossi wasn't being held in that place.

Mark made a quick survey of a second convalescent hospital that the Family had once owned, and again found nothing to arouse suspicion. His second potted flower went to a small girl with two broken legs who asked him if he were her uncle. He said he would like to be and left the flowers.

Before eleven o'clock, the Penetrator knocked on a door on the eighth floor of the Ritz Carlton Hotel, where Angie Rossi was supposed to be. To his surprise, she answered his knock with a delightful warm smile.

"Hey, am I glad to see you!" she said, reaching up and kissing his cheek. "Come in, come in. I've been going bananas sitting here with the damn TV set and six magazines. How much longer am I going to be locked up in here?"

"Maybe a week, so just relax," he said. She was beautiful. Her soft, clinging blouse let her breasts bounce delightfully when she moved. Her skirt was short and he was glad.

She saw his appraisal and shrugged.

"Sorry I'm not dressed; I didn't expect company." But her dark eyes showed a touch of approval. "At least not such a welcome guest. I promise I won't shoot at you." She laughed, closed the door, and led him into the living room of the suite. Clothes draped a chair and small table. It didn't bother her. She swept a magazine off the couch and sat down, patting a place beside her.

"Now, report in. What progress are we making?"

Mark grinned and watched her. "Not a hell of a lot," he said. He told her about the nursing home. "In any operation like this one, recon comes first, then intelligence takes over, and after we G-2 it the action phase starts."

"How's Monica?"

He told her about the visit last night, but nothing about his narrow escape.

Angie nodded. "Monica is a tough little wop; she'll

59

hold up. I just hope you didn't stir them up when they almost caught you there. They might move her."

"I don't think they will. They didn't know what I was looking for, and they don't know who I am. Now your job is to keep yourself buried here. Not a word to anyone, not even an old boyfriend. If the Family finds out you're here, they'll have to neutralize you too. And the traditional way is to perform a frontal lobotomy with a .45. You'd know in a flash their Tony wasn't Tony and you'd ask a batch of questions about your dad."

"Did you know he's seventy-three? Did you know that? He was almost fifty before I was born."

"How is he physically?"

"He never was in very good health. And if he's being kept sedated, those damn drugs could kill him."

"Then you be sure to stay put so we can move faster. Don't do anything to let any of the old bunch know you're in town. If you want to get out, put on a wig and some dark glasses and go for a drive; go see Tony. How did you register here?"

"Not under my own name. I knew something was strange when I got Tony's phone call." Her expression changed suddenly, fear crowding into her face, staining her eyes. "Is it going to be bad, Mark?"

"Some people are going to get hurt, Angie. I don't want you to be one of them. Someone always gets hurt in this kind of situation."

"Yes, you're right." She watched him. "Mark, tell me true, why are you here? A person doesn't fly three thousand miles and give up days and days of his time just to help out an old school friend he hasn't seen in five years. You didn't even know what the trouble was until you got here." She frowned. "Or shouldn't I ask why you're here?"

The Penetrator liked this girl. She was straight forward. "Angie, you can ask any question you want to."

"Why are you helping us?"

"Because you're my friends."

"Why are you carrying a gun?" She smiled. "I felt it when I leaned up to kiss you." She paused. "Are you a cop?"

She looked at him, waiting for an answer.

"Okay, Angie. I came because Tony was a friend. I also remembered his old man was a Mafia Don and I'm not on good terms with the Cosa Nostra. I did some combat work in Vietnam that trained me for the type of attacks we may need here to get Monica out of their prison. After I found out Tony's problem, I decided to follow through all the way."

"But are you a cop? Are you trying to put Tony or Daddy in jail?"

"No."

The smile that came over her face was like a birth of new spring blossoms. She reached up and kissed his cheek again.

"Good. I'm glad, Mark, because I did have that one little worry."

Mark watched her and sudden tenderness grew in him, only to be replaced with a longing he knew he had to put down fast. She was so damn attractive. . . . Mark stood.

She jumped up suddenly and they were standing close together. His hand brushed hers and then he pulled her into his arms and kissed her lips hard. She responded, then sighed and gently pushed him back.

Angie smiled, a gentle and winsome smile, as she took a step away. "Thanks, Mark. I was beginning to think maybe I would always be the kisser instead of the kissee."

Mark turned and forced himself to walk to the door.

"Sollozzo has brought in drugs; did you know that?" she asked him. "The Rossi family is now the biggest smuggler and pusher of heroin on the east coast. And Sollozzo has spawned a new racket here, Mark. He's opening up massage parlors with girls fifteen to seventeen. I can't bear to have anything like that associated with the Rossi name. I want him smashed, Mark, right down into the ground."

Her face was angry, then furious. "Daddy never let anything like that go on. Oh, I know, he was outside the law and all that. Yes, it was dirty money, but not that dirty! I want you to nail Sollozzo to one of his dirty rackets and stomp him into the ground!"

"Monica and little Tony have my first priority, Angie. If we can smother Sollozzo at the same time, I'll be more than happy to do it." He stepped back, looked at her again. "Do you have any money—without using your credit cards and blowing your cover?"

She looked up, surprised. "Wow, about twenty dollars, I guess. I hadn't thought about that."

Mark took out his billfold and gave her five one-hundred-dollar bills. She started to protest. "Don't worry about the money; it's a loan from Sollozzo, the numbers bank, remember?" Mark stepped back and looked her over carefully, staring at her. "I just don't understand it, Angie. How in hell can an ugly guy like Tony have such a beautiful sister?"

Angie smiled, reached up and kissed his lips once more, then opened the door. "I may decide to like you after all," Angie said as he went out the door.

Chapter Five

DEATH-SEAT KILL

The Penetrator sat in a booth in a dingy bar and poured another glass of beer for the man across from him. He had talked to over twenty skid row Charlies already. Most of them would spill their guts for the price of a beer, but enough of them had come across with the kind of information he hunted. Now Mark knew that the Boston Mafia had tightened up and toughened up since young Tony took over a year ago. Things were damned close right now.

One small-time pusher confessed that he had to chop his territory in half and pay twice as much for his junk now. One guy he knew didn't buckle under to the Family; he got his own stuff, and two days later they found him nailed to a wall with six-inch railroad spikes, spread-eagled, with the big nails through hands and feet. His guts had been ripped out and he died as slow and hard as any man ever had.

Mark concentrated on sometime sellers, small pushers, and he told them all the same story he gave this one.

"Look, friend, just between you and me, I'm going into business. Them damn Rossi horses' asses don't scare me. I got my own supply, top quality stuff. But I need contacts on the street, some hands to make connections, like at retail. So nose around, find me a dozen good leads and I'll make it worth your while. A quick thousand for you for every one that works out."

It was the tenth time he had gone through the speech, and Mark knew it would pay off. He had used the same bar, the same booth, and he figured that in two hours word would get to the top, and he'd have a caller.

Mark knew them as soon as they came through the door. Both were over six feet and wore twelve-dollar ties with small diamond tie tacks. Their suits were better than the average soldier's and their shaves close.

The first Mafia messenger drifted to the left, the second to the right, and before Mark had finished talking with the pusher in his booth, the big men had moved up and slid into the booth beside them. Mark felt a gun jam into his ribs. The weapon was hidden from sight. At least these guys were professionals.

Mark's own .45 prodded into the ribs of the man beside him, also under the table. The man was almost bald, with huge brown eyes over sagging bags of skin that ended in a thin, tight mouth.

66

Mark had both hands under the table top.

"Looks like we got ourselves a standoff," Mark said, looking at the man beside him. Both guns nudged harder.

Mark flexed his right arm, releasing the stiletto from its arm sheath. It came point first into his hand, and he took the handle as the guns pressed. He tilted the blade down and jammed it through the crotch of the man's pants letting it just nick flesh and stop.

"Baldy, you move so much as an inch and I'll slice your balls right down your pants leg. So just ease off on the hardware and put it on the seat between us."

"No way. . . ."

"You wanna talk falsetto the rest of your life?"

Slowly the pressure eased; the gun fell between them to the seat. Mark left it there.

"Tell your buddy to give his cannon to me with two fingers, over the top of the table."

The bald man, obviously the leader of the pair, nodded to his younger hoodlum companion. The kid swore under his breath, then pushed a Luger across the counter, then Mark holstered his .45 and pocketed it, also the weapon between them. He kept the knife where it was, increasing the pressure until Baldy moaned softly. Hatred was slanting from his eyes.

"Now stand up, junior, and walk into the latrine," he told the younger Mafia soldier. "You come out within ten minutes, your buddy here is turkey meat. Move!"

The man did as he was told, looking back, hatred burning in his eyes. Mark knew the goon had a hideout

67

weapon, but it wouldn't matter. By the time he vanished into the men's room, Mark had briefed Baldy on what to do. The Penetrator twisted the knife a little, then drew it out of the cloth and slid it back into its sheath. They stood and walked to the front door, then out into the cool of the Boston night. Mark slammed the pistol down across the soldier's forehead, leaving a trail of blood across his brow and cheek, then pushed the groggy man toward the LTD half a block ahead.

The Penetrator motioned for the soldier to get in from the driver's side and push over, which he did. Mark followed, the snubnosed .38 covering every motion.

Mark drove with one hand, the .38 always ready. As they rolled, Mark studied the Mafioso: maybe thirty-five, solid, a pro. It would be tough wringing any information from this one.

The man didn't say a word, wouldn't look at Mark. He stared out the side window. Mark slowed for a stopsign and came to a halt. A car pulled up beside him, and as Mark turned to look at the other rig, he saw the glint of a weapon. He jolted forward against the steering wheel, the plastic oval punching painfully into his rib cage.

At that instant the gun outside Mark's window went off and the other car roared away. Mark bounced back from the wheel into his seat and looked at his passenger.

The bullet intended for Mark had ripped through the Mafia button man's cheek, slanted upward, and traced some wild pattern through his brain tissue before it exited over his right ear, taking with it bits of skull, tissue, brain cells, and a gush of blood that splattered in red running lines down the side window. The bullet had continued through the window and lodged in a truck body next to Tony's rented LTD.

The light changed and Mark drove ahead quickly, turned off the highly traveled artery, and found a deserted alley. He checked to be sure the soldier was dead, then pushed him down out of sight and headed for the docks. It was well past working hours on most of the waterfront area.

Mark wasn't worried about being spotted. Although the shooting took place on a downtown street, half the people who heard the shot probably thought it was a backfire, the other half wouldn't know what it was, and if one or two had seen the actual killing, they had probably looked the other way, hoping they wouldn't be involved. He crept into the docks area and prowled until he found what he wanted: an unguarded dock with no railing.

The Penetrator waited beside a big pier building for an hour, then took a quick walk around the area. No one was there; nothing moved. It was a deserted part of the docks. He went back to check the LTD, taking everything from it that could tie him to it. Mark was glad he'd taken the weapons suitcase out the night before. He left the windows rolled down, started the engine, put the sedan in gear, and aimed it off the side of the pier. It went into the water with a splash, floated for thirty seconds, then vanished under the black waters of the bay. Mark froze against a piling, watching. No one ran to investigate. No outcry of alarm sounded. Mark moved from shadow to shadow as silently and stealthily as any of his Indian ancestors might have. Five minutes later he was away from the docks, running swiftly, silently through the deserted streets toward a blush of lights where he found a drug store, a phone, and soon a taxi.

Back at the Midtown Motor Inn Mark found Tony waiting for him. Tony snapped off the TV set and pushed the newspaper at Mark. It carried a big story about a local businessman who had been shot, beaten up, and left for dead on Carson Beach the evening before. Police were searching for a mystery man in connection with the attack; the victim had also been robbed of over two thousand dollars. A composite drawing was included, drawn according to the description given by the injured man. It showed a short, thick-set man with long blond hair, a beard, and blue eyes, wearing sandals, a fringed buckskin shirt, and blue jeans.

"You've changed," Tony said, indicating the picture.

"Tells you a lot about the Boston police," Mark said. "There was no way Primo could have ditched that heroin I planted. Some cop got there, took it for resale, and stripped him of his valuables. That's not too surprising, but how far up does the fix go? The Mafia soldier had been instructed to give a false report about his attacker. The Rossi family wants to deal with me in its own measured turkey-meat way."

Mark filled Tony in on his day's activities; then they talked for two hours about the Family mansion, where the power was concentrated, where Tony had grown up, and where Mike Sollozzo now must hold sway.

"Anything else I need to know? Like places of business they run, politicians Mike owns, anything?"

Tony rubbed his head a minute, thinking. These past two days had brought more color to his cheeks. Each day he swam in the pool and lay in the sun, soaking up the heat and getting the start of a suntan. He nodded.

"Yeah, I forgot about the boat, the *Anna Two*. She's a seventy-foot cruiser rigged for fishing. It's Dad's boat, but Mike used it the most; he's a nut about fishing. He might try to make it a hideout or make a run for it in the boat."

Mark thanked Tony, then made a call to the Boston police. Nobody was at the identification desk, so he talked to the watch sergeant.

"You'd better check your fingerprint file on one Tony Rossi. Check it against prints from the F.B.I. files. I can guarantee you they won't match." Mark hung up before the sergeant could put a trace on the call.

Tony looked at Mark curiously. "What's that all about?"

"Give them something to work on," Mark said. "And if they talk to Mike or to your ringer, they won't be able to spend so much time and manpower looking for me." Mark went over his mental bank of information about the Rossi operation. "Big Mike have any regular habits I should know about? Women, wine, this fishing?"

"Right," Tony said, remembering. "Mike used to go

71

fishing every Thursday morning, early. Today is Wednesday."

Two hours later they had moved out of the motel and settled in at the Fenway Boylston Motor Motel. The LTD had been rented with one of Mark's cover names, and he had used the same name at the motel. When the police found that car in the water with a fresh body in it, they would check out that rental name all over town.

When Mark had established their new identity and room, he called Angie to let her know where they were. He arranged for Tony to pick her up for a drive and lunch the next day.

For a half hour more Mark and Tony talked about where the Rossi boat should be moored, over on the Charles River at some place called the Storrow Drive Marina, and about all the details Tony could remember about the place.

"Sure you don't want me to go along tomorrow?" Tony asked.

Mark told him to rent another car and take a drive; then they turned in.

The next morning at six, Mark cruised the rented Pantera near the marina. It was what he expected, a sleek, guarded, quietly plush anchorage for very big and expensive boats.

Mark checked his arms. He had Ava, the updated version of the dart gun Professor Haskins had developed, which could spit darts containing knock-out juice or deadly poison; his favorite Colt Commander .45 tight in his clip-on holster at his right hip; the slender knife nestled neatly on his right arm and various small emergency equipment in his three-inch-wide belt. In his boots lay the small hypodermic needles and vials stocked with fresh drugs of several types.

Now all he had to do was get into the marina through the guarded gate. The posh Pantera couldn't be disguised as a delivery car. He'd have to chance it with a bluff. He rolled the car down to the gate and held the brake on as he gunned the powerful motor. The guard came up and Mark kept the rig moving slowly.

"Christ, get a move on, fart-head!" he shouted at the guard in his best downeast accent. "Big Mike said to get my fuckin' tail down here fast, so don't give me none of yer lip!"

The guard swallowed as Mark let his coat swing open, showing the .45 on his hip.

"Yes, sir. Go right on in. Mr. Sollozzo isn't here yet, but he should be along."

Mark gunned on through, leaving a patch of black tire rubber on the stop pad, and ground down to the high outline of the seventy-footer, *Anna Two,* that Tony had described for him in detail. She had a crew of three and this was Big Mike's fishing day. If the fish didn't bite, the men played cards and sometimes brought along a girl or two. Fishing had been good lately, so today Mark didn't expect they would have any doxies.

The Penetrator parked in a slot reserved for the boat two slips away from the *Anna Two* and changed into a blue-striped tee shirt and long-sleeved plaid shirt to go with his bell bottom jeans. He put on a black stocking cap, which was currently one of the trademarks of the boat crews in that part of the country.

Mark slipped on deck and was halfway to the bridge before anyone challenged him.

The man was crew, about twenty, wearing a black stocking cap and a red-striped tee shirt.

"Hey, man, what the hell you doing on board?" the crewman asked.

Mark shot him with Ava; the small, needlelike dart with its hypodermic nose caught the man in the side. The crewman pawed at the irritant for a second; then his body jolted with a series of spasms that rumbled through him for fifteen seconds, dropping him to the deck. At the end of that time he passed out from the M-99 and sodium pentothal mix in the hypo. He'd be unconscious for fifteen to twenty minutes.

Mark ran lightly up the steps to the bridge and caught the captain just as he reached into his jacket pocket.

Mark's side-hand slash jolted into the captain's neck over his right shoulder and he slumped to the deck, blinking back a rush of tears.

"What the hell? You come on board and just start hitting people?" the captain asked through the pain.

Mark pulled him to his feet, took the .32 revolver from his pocket, and pushed him into the high swivel stool. Then the Penetrator squatted by the rear wall and nodded to the skipper.

"Morning, Captain. You're going to sit right there, and when your passengers come, you'll cast off and get underway on your regular run, fishing, isn't it? You make one wrong move and you'll be bait for the blue sharks out there this morning." Mark waved the ugly muzzle of the Colt Commander .45 in the captain's direction.

"What . . . what's this all about?"

"You don't want to know, Captain. Just take us out to where Big Mike usually goes to fish; make it look as routine as hell."

"Big Mike isn't . . ."

Mark looked up quickly. "Sollozzo isn't coming today, right? But you're warmed up, ready to cast off. So you do have a party coming, and they are some of Mike's buddies?"

The captain looked out the cockpit without commenting. Mark knew he was correct. So he would still have two or three of the Rossi family to reason with. He watched the captain.

"You have a name?"

"Andrews."

"Okay, Captain Andrews, one of your crew is sick down by the aft ladder. Get your other crewman up there and stow him in a spare bunk."

The captain used his P.A. system to call the second crewman, who promptly took care of his unconscious buddy. It was all blamed on a wild night on the town.

Nearly half an hour passed before Mark heard a car drive up to the dock. Two men got out and came forward. Both wore suits, and they walked quickly, evidently anxious to get on board and out to the fishing banks. When they came up the small gangplank, both looked up at the bridge.

"Okay, Andrews, haul ass, the boss ain't comin' today. Get this scow in gear!"

Mark risked a look over the bottom edge of the window and saw a heavy-set man just over six feet. He wore a cowboy hat and thick glasses. The other passenger was shorter and slender. Both men went below, probably to change clothes, Mark decided, and Captain Andrews signalled for the lines to be cast off. A moment later the big boat's engines revved up and she pulled out through the marina and into the Charles River channel.

Mark nodded. So far everything was cool. They should sail down the river, out past Logan International Airport, and then he would take over. He wasn't sure how this would turn out, but he'd shake up the Mafia Don imposter. This would be a real fishing expedition for the Penetrator.

Chapter Six

A HOLE IN THE HEAD

Mark held his position behind the cabin partition, shielded from the rest of the ship and passengers, as the sleek craft worked its way down the broad roads to the sea; he was content to wait until they were well into the edge of the Atlantic before he made his move. Just past Deer Island he heard the two guests on the deck below him. One called to the captain, who slowed the *Anna Two* to five knots as the men dropped over trolling jigs.

The captain looked down at Mark. "They do that every time. I tell them there's nothing on the surface this time of year in here, but they keep trying."

The Penetrator shrugged. "I've got all day; just keep them happy. Where's your other crewman?"

"In the galley getting my breakfast and something for our *friends* down there."

Mark looked at the man's expression. His tone had let slip traces of concealed disgust.

"You're not one of the team, Captain?" Mark watched him thinking it through, then waver. He was about forty-five, spreading a little at the waist, his face weathered and tanned as only the sea can do it.

"I'm a boatman, a fisherman. Had my own commercial boat for years, then went into sport fishing. I know every shoal and bank within two hundred miles of that light."

Mark looked up as a form came through the door to the bridge cabin, surprise flooding the visitor's face. It was the smaller of the two hoods. Ava hissed; the man grabbed his stomach where the small, needle-nosed dart jammed into his flesh. He had time only to look at Mark before he fell inside the cabin, his body writhing and jerking spasmodically, twisting him beyond any possible conscious effort as his muscles cramped. Before Mark had pulled him the rest of the way into the cabin, the small man was unconscious.

The Penetrator took a roll of thirty-pound monofilament fishing line from his pocket and tied the man's ankles, then his hands behind his back. Mark watched the captain during the proceedings, but saw no sudden movements.

"Captain Andrews, how many radio microphones do you have on board?"

"Just one, all I need."

Mark took the mike and jerked it, tearing loose the wires, and threw it in a drawer. "Leave it there, Captain; it'll help you explain all this to Big Mike." Mark stepped toward the door and paused, still out of sight of the deck. "Sorry about your breakfast, Captain, but it's going to be delayed."

They had passed the lighthouse and bulled through the first few angry Atlantic swells; then they were in the heavy chop of the boisterous ocean as the craft moved east.

"Where were you going to fish today, Captain?"

"Three-mile reef is what I figured."

"Keep going there."

Mark slid down the ladder, saw the two trolling poles in holders on the stern and the jigs bouncing along a hundred yards behind. Where was the big guy? With Ava in one hand, Mark crept toward the steps near the center of the craft which led down to the galley and sleeping area. At once he smelled coffee and bacon. Near the bottom of the steps Mark paused. Two men sat at one of the tables. The heavy one still wore his cowboy hat but now had on blue jeans jacket and pants. The crewman had a dish towel wrapped around his waist and was working on a cup of coffee.

Mark remembered the first crewman he had seen. The two men faced away from him, so Mark drifted four feet to the short companionway and into the first room. The crewman he had darted with Ava stood in the center of the room, rubbing his head. Mark showed him the .45 and put a finger to his lips.

"If you want to live more than ten seconds, stay quiet and lie down on the bunk."

The crewman, no more than eighteen, nodded, his eyes wide with fear and surprise. He nodded again.

Mark tied his hands and feet with more of the heavy fishing mono and put a red kerchief around his mouth.

"Now stay put and live to be an old sailor with a long white beard."

Mark checked the companionway, retraced his steps, and walked up to the pair in the galley before they noticed him.

"Breakfast ready?" Mark asked.

When the big man saw Mark, he fumbled at his belt. Mark caught him on the neck with a side-of-the-hand chop, driving him off the stool and to the floor. His hand found his own weapon, which Mark kicked away from him.

"Get up," Mark barked. He looked the crewman back into his chair. "Both of you, hands locked on top of your head, now!" The kid, about twenty, quickly joined his hands and kept them on his head. "This guy have a name?" Mark asked the crewman. The kid nodded. "Spill it!"

The crewman looked at the man on the floor, then at the .45 Mark held in his hand.

"Canzonari, Louis Canzonari."

"Get up, Louis, you and me got a date on deck." Mark looked at the crewman, another sheep, an innocent.

"Kid, you like living?"

"Yeah."

"What?"

"Yes, sir!"

"Some guys don't, like Canzonari here. You ever seen a man die, kid?"

80

"No, sir."

"You want to be involved with this?"

"No . . . no, sir."

"Which cabin has an outside lock on the door?"

"Number three, the storeroom."

"Get in it, now," Mark said, prodding Canzonari to his feet. He locked the crewman in the room, then kicked Canzonari on deck. They were still heading east at ten knots. Mark searched the Mafioso, then put away his own weapon. "You ever boxed, Canzonari? Are you a fighter?"

The hood came running at Mark like a pile driver. Mark waited until his hands had almost closed, then jumped to one side and smashed his double fists down on the unprotected back of the man's neck. Canzonari went down to one knee, skidded into the bait tank, then surged to his feet, furious.

He came slower this time, charging at the last moment. Mark didn't move; he timed it perfectly and kicked the big man in the stomach, dove to his left, rolled, and came back on his feet as Canzonari screamed, fell to the deck, and vomited. The Mafia soldier shook his head, his eyes bleary, as he stared at the pale green fluids he had disgorged; then he threw up again. At last he pushed to his feet.

"Bastard, I'll kill you for that!" Canzonari shouted.

A knife came into his hand, and Mark had a good look at it. It was a fish filleting knife, the eight-inch blade sharpened so often it was barely half an inch wide, but strong and sharp enough to slice through shark skin.

"You could get hurt with a blade, Canzonari. All I want from you is some information."

The soldier charged, feinted left, drove ahead, then sprang to one side, but missed the slash at Mark's stomach. The Penetrator let Canzonari watch the stiletto slide down his arm into his hand, then stepped in. Mark drove him back past the bait tank, beyond the life rafts to the stern rail.

Canzonari wasn't used to knife fighting. He'd relied too long on his lead-spitting .38. But he made one last try, charging ahead, darting to one side, then swinging hard and kicking out at the same time. Mark parried the knife blade with the stiletto, kicked hard at the on-coming foot, and upended the hoodlum, the knife jolting from his hand as he fell.

"Man overboard!" Mark yelled, and at once the throbbing diesels below decks cut off. Mark pulled the Mafia leader up by his jacket front, slapping his face with one hand, then, reversing his motions, half-car-ried, half-propelled Canzonari toward the stern rail. He bent him over the mahogany plank, one of his big hands pressing in on Canzonari's throat.

"I've got some questions, soldier. You ready to an-swer them?"

There was no reaction from the hoodlum.

"You a good swimmer, Canzonari? We're about two miles from the nearest bit of land."

Terror darted through the Mafia man's face, then vanished.

"I swim like a fish."

"Two miles?"

Canzonari lunged up the deck, but Mark caught him with what could have been a perfect waist-high down-field block. Instead, Mark grabbed his victim, surged upward, carried him to the side rail, and in one continuous movement launched Canzonari over the side.

He didn't even go underwater. In total fright, his arms and legs threshed the water so hard as he hit that his head never went out of sight. His scream was one of terror that could not be disguised.

Captain Andrews came to the side of the bridge, reaching for a life-saving ring, but Mark shook his head.

"Canzonari, something big is going down at the mansion. I want to know exactly what it is. Tell me all about it."

"Christ, throw me a life ring and I'll tell you. I can't swim!"

"Tell me now, Canzonari."

The boat drifted away from him and Canzonari floundered in the water, trying to move toward the boat. It was all he could do to stay up. He worked his way closer, dog paddling. Mark took a gaff hook from the bait tank cross arm and showed Canzonari the sharp steel hook on the end. "Want to get gaffed, big man?" Mark asked, splashing the water in front of him. "Or do you want to wait for that shark right out there to get hungry?"

"Shark? What shark?" Canzonari sputtered. "Where, for God's sake?"

"Coming. What's happening up in the mansion?

What's the big action? Spill your guts, Canzonari, or the gaff and that shark will do it for you."

A look of cunning touched his face. "Shit, man, you wouldn't leave me out here."

"Goodbye, Canzonari. Half speed, Captain; let's head back for port." Captain Andrews did as he was told without a backward glance at the hoodlum.

Canzonari screamed, his words quickly drowned out by the gutteral rumble of the twin diesels below deck. The *Anna Two* pulled away a hundred yards, until Mark couldn't see the man as he dropped into a trough; then Mark motioned to the captain, who turned the fisher around and headed back to the spot they had left.

It took five minutes to find Canzonari. He was exhausted from just trying to stay afloat. Mark threw him a life ring, then one end of a coil of half-inch rope. The Penetrator tied his end of the line to the stern rail. Canzonari came toward them, pulling himself in.

"Ready to talk now, big man?" Mark asked.

Canzonari shook his head.

Mark splashed water in front of him with the gaff, its bright, four-inch-long steel point glistening in the sunshine. The underworld soldier stopped.

Canzonari cried and shook his fist. "Dammit to hell. Let me on board; then I'll talk."

Mark shook his head this time. "I want all of it, now." He held up his hand to the captain. "Ten knots, Andrews, heading back to sea. Let's see how good a water skier our boy is without his skis."

Canzonari screamed when he felt the boat move, the

line draw tight and then start dragging him through the water. He knew he should laugh at this maniac, swear at him, and get back on board and grind him down into turkey meat—but he was much too terrified. Water had always scared him; deep water made him panic. The boat went faster. A sheet of salt water slapped him in the face. He almost lost his grip on the life ring. Then he went under. Canzonari knew he tried to scream down there, but he only gagged on more foul-tasting salt water and was half drowned before he came up. The water slashed at him as the boat seemed to go faster and faster. His feet trailed out behind now, and he found that by spreading his legs he could stay upright. All the time he was cursing the man on board. Who was he? How did he know they would be here? Canzonari lost his precarious perch on the water and fell off to his side, the water snapping his head back, rolling him under again. The guy would push and push until only his .45 cannon was left; then it would be a knee or maybe his crotch, and at last his head.

Canzonari wanted to give up and die right then, but somehow he couldn't force his fingers off the lifesaving ring. Death grip. He thought only about a death grip as he came to the surface again and realized they had stopped, that he was bobbing in the water.

The solid steel of the gaff touched Canzonari's arm. Now he knew it couldn't be a dream.

"What's your name?" Mark asked.

"Louis Canzonari."

"Who do you work for?"

"Big Mike Sollozzo."

"Not for Don Antonio Rossi?"

"Oh, yeah, for him too."

"Are you the number three man or number four for Big Mike?"

"Three."

"Something big is going down soon; what is it?"

"White casket. The damn white casket caper. Now let me on board!"

"What's the white casket play, Canzonari?"

"Who knows? Heard them talking about it. Some damn casket coming to bury the old man in. Old Don Carlo, only it ain't just a casket. I don't know what else, for Christ's sake."

"When's it coming, Canzonari?"

"They said three days, maybe a week. Now get me on board, dammit!"

Mark pulled him in closer, let him hold onto the railing at the side of the boat near the stern scupper. A short gaff now poised in the air over the man. "Where are you keeping Don Carlo? Where do you have him on ice?"

Canzonari laughed. "Christ, wouldn't you like to know."

Mark gaffed him in the upper arm, the sharp point thrusting upward through the muscles and tissues, grazing the bone and almost coming out the top of Canzonari's heavy arm.

The hoodlum screamed again and again until he choked down the pain to a blubbering whine. He held on with one hand, and Mark reversed the force on the gaff and jerked it downward out of the arm the way he would release gamefish on the deck.

"Where are you holding Don Carlo?"

Canzonari almost passed out. Mark dropped the gaff and bent, grabbing the hoodlum's good arm, holding him against the *Anna Two* as she rocked gently in the Atlantic swells.

"Where is he?" Mark shouted at the glazed eyes.

"Continental Gardens Sanitarium," Canzonari said. His eyes cleared and he looked at Mark. "Christ, don't ever tell anybody who told you or I'll be a dead man."

"You positive that's where the old man is?"

"Yeah, shit yeah!"

"And he's on drugs, to keep him knocked out?"

"Right, and in pain. Damn, he's got cancer of something and he's in bad shape."

"Thanks, Canzonari, and goodbye."

The big .45 slug took Canzonari squarely in the throat, blasting his windpipe into splinters, hurtling on through his neck, disintegrating the finely constructed stack of bones, and snuffing out his life in a hundredth of a second. When the slug came out of the man's neck it was misshapen and bloody, and dragging a length of small artery as it splashed into the Atlantic, sinking quickly toward the bottom in sharp contrast to the slow descent of Louis Canzonari's remains. He drifted down a dozen feet, where a current caught him and carried him toward the open sea. An eight-foot blue shark saw the strange form, cruised by it once, then moved up cautiously and bumped it with its snout. Was it something to eat? The shark circled around and began its attack.

On board the *Anna Two* Mark felt a small muscle in his jaw tighten. Another Mafia cutthroat cashed in. Canzonari had made his death pact years before when he took the Mafia pledge; his fate had just been a little slow in catching up with him. Mark looked at the bridge and saw Captain Andrews watching him. Before he could speak, a second face appeared beside the captain and a hand with a small gun came up and fired.

Mark had no time to aim. His .45 lifted and blasted as he relied on his remarkable eye-hand coordination to set his computer. He missed. He had instinctively aimed for the hoodlum's chest; instead the 200-gram slug went wide and shattered the man's upper right arm, jolting the .32 out of his hand, dumping him bloody and wailing against the captain's chair.

Five seconds later, Mark was at the bridge door. The captain's face was grim.

"He's bleeding to death," Captain Andrews said.

Mark stared at him for a moment. The captain was a good man, a sheep, a damned civilian who wasn't a bad guy, but sure as hell not a good guy. He was one of the floaters in between, trying to keep his head above water.

Mark took a towel and made a tourniquet around the shattered upper arm and stopped the bleeding.

"Let's get back to port, Captain, but don't use the radio."

Mark carried the wounded man down the steps to

the hatch cover and spread him out. He was still unconscious, but breathing normally. The bleeding had stopped, so he would live.

Mark checked the two crewmen. They were below, pounding on the doors, mad as hell but alive. He left them there.

Back on the bridge, he watched the captain.

"You'll have to report this to the Coast Guard," Mark said. "You lost a man overboard and this one shot himself cleaning his .32. Be sure you tell them it was a .32."

The captain shook his head. "Not me. I'm not reporting any of this. You think the Rossis will let me go on piloting this boat for them now?" He shook his head. "I wondered why this job paid so well. Now I know. It might be the last job a captain ever has."

Just after they passed Deer Island, Andrews motioned to Mark. "Bulgosi, he's the shot-up one. He made me untie him. He knows where I live. Said he'd take care of my wife good unless I cut him loose." The captain watched for Mark's reaction. "Said he'd get my wife, attack her, then use a knife on her. You know what a guy like him can do. So I cut him loose. He fixed the radio mike and called shore, some kind of a radio telephone patch-in."

Mark listened to that information with a frown. "So they'll have some heavyweight welcoming party back at the dock when we get there, all ready, primed and waiting for us, right?"

Captain Andrews began to sweat. "Right," he said.

Chapter Seven

THE DARTS OF DEATH

Mark watched the blue-green water slide under the bow as he thought about what would be waiting for them at the dock. It wasn't a matter of deciding whether to go back; obviously they couldn't walk into a shooting gallery like that. But what should be his next move?

By the time they sailed into the Charles River, Mark had it worked out. He had Captain Andrews put the big boat in at a public pier and tie her up. The Penetrator jumped off the craft as soon as she touched dock, sprinted down a block to the street, and kept right on going. Ten minutes later he eased into a phone booth.

A half hour after that, Tony picked him up from a small restaurant. Angie had come along for the ride.

"So what happened to your Pantera?" Tony asked as soon as Mark slid in beside Angie in the front seat.

"Tony, you should join the diplomatic corps. You'd fit right in. Not hello, how are you. No; just what happened to the Pantera."

Tony snorted and said something in Italian. "Okay already. How are you? Hello. Now, what the hell happened to that rented Pantera you drove down there?"

Mark told them what the morning's fishing expedition had produced, except for the dialogue about their father. That he had to hold for the right time.

"White casket?" Angie asked, her nose twitching. "That doesn't make much sense. Why would anyone want to bring in a white casket?"

"That's what we're going to find out."

"When do we go in and get Monica and little Tony?" Tony asked.

"As soon as we can, buddy. Just as soon as we get Sollozzo set up. We have to push him off balance. If we try to move in now, he throws a hundred gorillas at us in five minutes. Those aren't good odds."

"So we wait," Angie said. "Mark knows what he's doing."

Tony looked at his sister as he drove; his frown softened and at last he nodded.

"Okay, Miss Italy, we wait."

"Was your father ever sick much? Have any long-lasting problems?" Mark asked.

"Iron Man Rossi?" Tony yelped. "He used to tell us he never even got a cold. Not the flu or coughs, none of that stuff bothered him. He was solid as a rock."

"You heard something about him?" Angie asked.

"One of the guys I talked with said your father was sick, besides the drugs they have him on. Said he was very sick."

"So let's get him out first," Tony said.

Mark watched Tony driving smoothly through the heavy morning traffic. "No, he isn't the first priority. We go in for him when I'm sure we can get him out alive. It has to be the right time, tactically."

"So when, dammit? I'm getting tired of waiting."

Angie reached across Mark and touched Tony's arm. "Tony, easy. You've waited three years; what's another few days going to hurt?"

"Okay, okay. How about an early lunch then? Let me win at something."

Tony picked a small eatery off the main streets where no one Angie knew would go. But she left her big sunglasses on just in case. They ordered, and before the food came, Tony went to the men's room.

Angie looked at Mark seriously. "Mark, I want to thank you for what you're doing for Tony, for all of us. You're a most unusual person, a very special man."

"You're just telling me that so I'll pick up the check," Mark said, trying to change the serious tone of the conversation. He held up his hand as she protested. "Okay, that's noted in the records." He watched her dark eyes, wondering what made them sparkle that way, even with her sunglasses on. She was smiling at him and suddenly he felt as though he wanted to take her pretty face in his hands and kiss her.

"Mark, what are you thinking about?"

93

"What? Thinking about? Were my hunger pangs showing?"

"I don't know; the way you smiled, and your eyes went kind of dreamy ... it seemed ... mysterious. I bet you're a Virgo."

"A what? No, not likely, but I don't fool around with that astrology stuff."

Her small hand touched his; he looked down at the long, slender fingers and carefully clear-polished nails. "Maybe you should get into it; it might be fun."

Mark laughed, realizing he enjoyed her hand on his. "I've got trouble enough just doing what I've got going now."

Tony came back and the food arrived.

A half hour later they drove up to the Ritz Carlton and Angie got out. She paused at the door, looking down.

"Mark, could you come up for a few minutes? I've got something I want to talk to you about."

"Goddamn, I knew it," Tony said softly.

Mark looked at Tony. "The only thing I've planned for the rest of the day should go down about ten tonight. You want to go out and play banker again with me?"

Tony brightened. "Damn right!"

"Good. I'll be back at the motel before long. Why don't you get some sun around the pool?"

Tony looked at Angie, then chuckled. "What the hell, I guess I can't protect Mark forever. He's old enough to know about girls."

Mark laughed and got out, closed the door, and

waved as Tony spun the car's wheels getting away from the curb.

A few minutes later in her room, Angie turned on some music and smiled at Mark. "I didn't want to tell Tony, but I had word about a year ago that Daddy has cancer. It started in one leg and they amputated it at the knee and thought they had stopped it. Then about four months ago one of the men's wives wrote and told me I should come home, that Daddy was very sick again. I don't know what the situation is now."

She sat on the sofa suddenly and blinked, fighting back tears. He sat beside her, and when she leaned toward him he put his arms around her.

"If you've known about it for this long, Angie, you know there's only one outcome you can expect."

She nodded, the tears coming, and Mark didn't try to stop them. She pushed closer against him and he held her, letting the tears wash away some of the sadness. Slowly the sobs trailed off and she wiped her eyes.

"I didn't mean to start crying," she said, looking up. "But it's been a long time since I felt secure enough with someone that I could cry. I know that makes lousy sense, but sometimes I need a good cry."

Mark bent and kissed her forehead. "I think it makes a lot of sense. I just cry inside. Everyone needs someone."

She looked up. "Thanks. Now would you mind aiming that kiss a little lower?"

Mark did and he heard her sigh as their lips met. A moment later she pulled away, then snuggled close to him. "You'll find out that I'm a very direct person, Mark. I'm a little pushy, but that's because I was spoiled as a child and I haven't quite got the remodeling job done yet, but I'm working on it. I'm over twenty-one, I like wine better than whiskey, I take my shower in the evening, hate skiing, and I drink gallons of coffee."

She reached up and kissed his lips gently.

"Besides that, you're a little crazy," he said. "How do you think Tony is standing the pressure of coming home?"

"Fine. Tony is a little psyched up, but he'll be okay. He's one hell of a tough wop. Those aborigines couldn't stop him, and neither can a *puto* like Mike Sollozzo."

Mark bent and kissed her, harder this time, more demanding, and they slid lower on the big sofa.

"If we mess around and I fall off here and break my arm, I'm gonna sue you," Angie said.

Mark broke up laughing. When he stopped he touched her nose with his finger.

"Look, about your father . . ."

She shook her head, stopping him. "No. First we worry about Monica and little Tony. The family— remember, we Italians are very family-centered. The young ones are most important; they are the future of the family line. We worry most about little Tony, then about Monica, then Daddy."

"You are a tough little wop."

She stuck her tongue out at him.

"Want some coffee?"

"Not really."

"Okay. Now about that white casket thing. Could it be for Daddy?"

Mark stood and walked to the window; he looked out over Boston, shaking his head. "I don't see why. A big operation for a special casket? That doesn't make sense even for a Don. There has to be more to it than that. There may not be a box at all. That may be just a code word. Then again there might be a very expensive casket coming. It could be a code word having something to do with death. I've even heard heroin called 'the white death.' That's not too far from white casket. We'll just have to wait and find out."

Mark walked toward the door. "I better start doing some of my homework. I'll take a raincheck on that coffee."

"I'll cry but you can go." Angie pouted for a moment, then walked to him and stretched up. "At least I should get three goodbye kisses."

"You are a spoiled brat," Mark said, but reached down and kissed her. "Now, you remember to stay inside unless you wear your disguise. We've got to keep your little visit here a secret for a few more days."

"I promise." She kissed him once more and walked him to the door. "You and Tony going to try to knock over a numbers bank tonight?"

"Right; you pick up on things fast."

"Good luck, and ... *don't you dare get in the way of any stray bullets.*" She turned and walked away, her anger growing.

"Hey, I'll try, I'll try," Mark said.

She refused to turn around.

"Just get out of here, go play your damn male bang-bang games!"

Mark left, caught a taxi back to the motel, and found Tony cleaning his .45. He looked up.

"Okay, what's Angie's big secret? She tell you the old man has cancer?"

"Right; how did you know?"

"It figured. He'd have to be damn bad off before Mike could even try for a bloodless coup. Who we busting tonight?"

That night just after ten, Mark and Tony went up a rear fire escape and moved on sneakers silently across a flat roof. Both wore navy blue pants and shirts. Using two suction cups and a glass cutter, Mark swiftly removed an eight-inch square of glass, reached in and pulled the latch, and opened one side of the skylight. Inside it was dark. Mark aimed his pocket flash downward to the floor. He rigged a small pulley on the skylight frame, tested it, then slid quarter-inch nylon line through it and let himself into the void. Fifteen feet below he jumped onto the loft floor. Tony followed, then pulled down the cord.

Both moved cautiously through the room and down a dusty, unused hallway to a set of steps. They placed their feet on the very sides of the stair tread as they worked their way downward without a squeak. On the first floor they found lights at the back of the building.

Mark had emphasized that this must be a silent hit. He had Ava primed and ready with six deadly curarine poison darts. Tony carried Mark's silenced .45, a knife, and a wicked leather-covered sap.

The room they wanted was locked from the inside, but as usual the counters would open it for the little Chinese who brought them free Chinese food about this time every night. They found the right door; then Mark gave the tap, tap, pause and two more taps, the signal that the food had come.

They heard a chair scrape back and feet plod toward the door; then two bolts were pulled and a hasp was thrown back. The door was hinged on Mark's right and opened inward, so Mark stood slightly to the right of the doorknob. He would be able to see inside the moment the door cracked open.

The Mafia soldier unlatched the door and pulled it in two inches, trying to see into the dimly lit hall. He swore and moved the door open farther.

Ava hissed; the dart rammed through two layers of shirt and undershirt, stabbing its hollow needle a quarter of an inch into the hood's chest. Mark leaped ahead, hitting the door with his shoulder, smashing it open, and surged into the room. He snapped two quick shots with Ava at another man, who looked up from a card table stacked with bundles of paper money.

The first dart missed, but the second hit the hoodlum in the neck, the steel dart penetrating half an inch into the pliant flesh, where the curarine gushed out and began its swift message of death to the central nervous system.

Both men were dead before Mark and Tony got to the table. No one else was there. Tony took a folded plastic sack from his pocket, snapped it open, and scraped the piles and bundles of bills into it. He bent and took a .38 revolver from one of the corpses. The rest of the room was bare. Mark dropped a two-inch-long Indian blue flint arrowhead on each body. Tony looked at him questioningly; then they both ran to the hall, went down its dusty, dark length, and kicked open a locked door leading to the alley.

Twenty minutes later they were back at the Fenway Boylston Motel with the chain lock on the door. Tony began counting the pile of money.

He paused, looked up, his face courting a frown.

"Hey, Mark, you just wasted two men tonight. You killed them dead. No regrets?"

It was Mark's turn to frown. It was a question he had asked himself a hundred times. His answer was always the same.

"No, Tony, no regrets. Absolutely none. Those two were the dregs of society, leeches, hired killers, white slavers. They live off the depravity, the suffering, the pain of others. They don't deserve to live. They can't be classified as men. They're animals, and the world is a better place without them."

"And they're Mafia," Tony said. "Isn't that part of the reason you came to help me, thinking you might be able to cut up a Mafia operation?"

"I didn't think about it at the time. But since I'm in the neighborhood . . ."

"My father is one of them, Mark."

The Penetrator nodded slowly as he stared back at Tony. "Yes, Tony, but he's an old man; from what we have heard he's terminally ill. He has blood up to his elbows, as you know. But my vengeance against the Cosa Nostra isn't personal, and it isn't all black or all white. Your father has suffered a. thousand deaths in the past year. If I can smash the Rossi family organization here I'll do nothing to harm your father."

Tony looked up and nodded, but Mark couldn't read his face.

Chapter Eight

HAVE A BLAST!

Tony Rossi stood, walked slowly to the window, then came back rubbing his face with one hand.

"Mark, I don't like what the Mafia is doing here in town any better than you do. Especially since it's all done in my father's, now in *my name*. I'll help you every way I can to blast them, to destroy the Mafia machine here in Boston. I'm with you right up to the point where my wife and son are in danger because of what I'm doing." He nodded as if agreeing with himself. "Now, what's next?"

Mark felt a surge of admiration for his friend. He had guts and he wasn't afraid to fight. That would help. Mark went through his mental hit list of jobs needing to be done. The top item on the list said "White Casket."

"How well do you know the layout of the Family

mansion? Could you get us inside and up to the offices where Big Mike is?"

"With my eyes closed and boots on."

"Quietly. Could you go through their alarm system?"

Tony shook his head. "I don't know much about electronics, and Dad used to have a complicated setup of alarms. They changed them every month. Dad said it was for our own protection, which meant mostly for his protection. I don't know what new sophisticated gear they might have installed in there now. You won't get inside by jumping over a wall or swinging down from a tree."

Mark narrowed his eyes. He had been afraid of this. "Then how about our going in through the front gate?"

Tony looked up, puzzled.

It was a little after midnight when Tony and Mark lounged against their rented car in a street six blocks from the Rossi family mansion. It was a stop street and the main "getting home" route for the Mafia soldiers on a shift change.

One of the big Caddy crew wagons drifted past, but it had two men in it. The next one came five minutes later with only a driver. Tony began walking across the street and banged into the side of the black Caddy just as it slowed to a crawl for the stop sign. The driver jammed on the brakes, rammed open the door, and came out of the car swearing.

"What the hell ya doing, you stupid kid? Dammit, if

you scratched her paint your asshole ain't gonna shit for a week!"

As the driver came around the back of the car, Mark's .45 butt slammed down hard on his head. The man whimpered once, then fell to the pavement. They tied his hands and feet and dumped him in the back seat of the rented car. Mark got in the driver's side of the Caddy and Tony slumped in the back as if sleeping.

Mark pulled up at the cul-de-sac that led to the mansion and put the Caddy's bumper an inch from the big steel gate. The Mafia soldier on duty was half asleep when he came out of the little gate house and stared at the car, then at Mark.

"Yeah?"

"Open up the goddam gate, stupid. You wanta engraved invite maybe?"

"Who the hell are you?" the gate man asked.

"Joe Hammer from Philly, dumbass! Now open up the damn gate, I got Tony in here."

The guard shifted his flashlight to Tony, sacked out in the back seat.

"Damn, that's him. But he came through two hours ago."

"So he went out again; you gonna wake him up and tell him he can't do that?"

"Hell no!" The guard shook his head, went back to the gatehouse, and pushed the switch that swung the heavy barricade inward. Mark wheeled the Caddy up a winding drive to a six-car garage next to a three-story massive stone mansion. He parked in the end slot of the garage and cut the light. Tony scrambled out of the car and touched Mark's shoulder.

"This way," Tony said, gliding like a shadow through the building to a door at the far end. A stairway led upward. It was narrow, dimly lighted, and looked little used.

"This gets us to the second floor where the offices are," Tony said. "The Family used to live on the third floor, with the barracks rooms and offices on two. Probably still that way."

Mark was ready to pass himself off as a Mafia soldier. He and Tony had decided his best chance would be the crew quarters, a combination day room and sleeping area. He should be able to pick up enough chatter there about the white casket without trying to brave Big Mike in his den. Tony looked out a door on the second-floor landing, and closed it gently.

"Yeah, this is the place. Two doors down on the right should be the target unless Big Mike has switched a lot of things around. Inside should be double-deck bunks, a pool table, two or three TV sets, a refrigerator or two, and a small kitchen. Go in and do your thing."

Mark gave Tony the keys to the car. "If anything goes sour, you get that Caddy and ram it out the front gate. It isn't strong enough to stop the Cadillac, and you should be able to drive for a mile even if the radiator gets smashed. Just keep plowing along to the rental car. Don't worry about me; I'll get out. If you hear any shooting, you haul ass out of here fast!"

Tony nodded.

Mark adjusted his dark suit and light blue shirt with wild tie and worked up a snarl. He went into the hall and headed for the crew quarters as if he'd been there a thousand times. When he opened the door his attitude was casual bordering on indifference. But his eyes were alert; he took in everything at a glance and recorded it for possible later use. He was stripping off his tie as he moved toward the big coffee urn at the near side. Six men were in bunks. The lights were down at that end of the room. Both TV sets flickered at him. Two men looked up, shrugged, and went back to girlie magazines.

Mark took a cup of java and slumped down in a chair near the hood with the *Playboy*.

"God—damn! You seen the pussy in that one, the big centerfold? Now there is a woman. I mean she's got it all and she shows you, the old beaver shot, the whole damn thing!"

The hood reading the magazine lowered it and growled.

"Buddy, when I get there, I'll look. Now butt out!"

"You trying for a busted mouth, you sad sonofabitch?" Mark said, his voice low but with a viciousness that was unmistakable. The other man pulled back.

"Who the hell are you?" he asked meekly.

"Hammer, up from Philly for the big deal. When the hell is it busting loose, anyway?"

"Hammer? Never heard of you."

"Never heard of you either, weirdo." Mark moved over to the far TV set and sat beside another Mafia mufti soldier. This one was watching Judy Garland skip down a yellow brick road.

"Hey, who the hell's the broad, Linda Lovelace?" Mark asked.

The soldier looked over, irritated. He had a sloping forehead and small eyes. He stared at Mark for a moment, then shook his head. "Naw, dummy. Don't you know nothing? That's Dorothy. She's going to see the big boss, the *capo*, out there at the end of the road in the land of Oz."

Mark snorted, walked to the pool table. So far he had drawn a real blank. He had just run four balls in a row, including a bank shot in the side pocket, when a redhead with a scar over one eye challenged him.

"Who the hell are you?"

"Hammer from Philly, and I'll be glad when this chicken operation is over. When the hell is it coming off?"

"Damned if I know. The casket biggie?"

"Yeah." Mark shot again, a combination with the two off the six, sliding the two into the side pocket. "I got some heavy-duty work coming up down south. They could have told me how damn long I'm gonna be nailed down up here. Where's Bulgosi, I'm going to get some answers."

The redhead held his cue against Mark's chest with one hand on each end. "Hold it, man, or you'll get your ass burned. Just relax and cool it; let's shoot some pool. How about a buck a ball?"

Mark kept his scowl on.

"Bulgosi can't help you, Hammer; he's in the hospital. Got himself shot up some. And we got a score to settle for that one. But don't worry about the damn white casket. It's all set and smooth. Within the next three days it's coming. Cocaine, from what I hear, but I ain't supposed to know. It's all hidden away in that damned expensive white casket. Neat, huh?"

Mark watched as the redhead ran three balls in a row, all stripes. The man could shoot pool.

"Three more days in this damn place and I'll go bananas," Mark growled.

"Remember the bonus and it's a hell of a lot easier," the redhead said. "And no sweat with the feds. I mean they can't inspect every fishing boat that comes in from a day out on the banks, can they? We'll waltz in right under the damned Coast Guard's nose."

"Yeah, great. But I'd rather be back in Philly where I know what's going on." Mark put up his cue. "Hang in there, Mack, and get all you can." He turned and headed for the door. Mark expected someone to stop him. His hand was near his .45, but the call never came. He faded through the door and into the hallway. Mark had what he came for, but he didn't want to go without leaving a calling card. He walked along the corridor, listening, but heard nothing he could use in any way. He moved to the back stairs and found Tony leaning against the wall.

"So?"

"I got the details; now where would they keep their arsenal? Extra guns, ammo, maybe some dynamite?"

Tony grinned. "A little farewell package?"

Mark nodded.

"It's over the garage. It used to be locked and guarded."

"Good; I'm getting tired of being nice to these Mafia goons."

They found the room a few moments later. There was no guard. Mark bent over the lock, opening it with a plastic credit card from his wallet. Inside, he took a pocket flash and a small pencil-type timer from his pocket. They found the ammunition and ten sticks of dynamite in one corner in a cardboard box.

With that as a base, Mark piled boxes of ammunition and a dozen high-powered rifles on the stack. He set the timer fuse for five minutes and waved Tony out the door. They strolled down the stairs, talked for a moment with a man driving in, then stepped into the Caddy they had used before and backed it out.

"So far, so good," Tony said as they made it halfway to the gate in the big car.

Behind them a bright orange flash sliced through the darkness, followed by a thundering rumble as the package over the garage went off.

Tony turned and saw the garage wing disintegrate in the glare of the security floodlights. The second-story roof lifted half a dozen feet, then dropped and carried the rest of the building, smashing, crushing downward on the five big cars below. A fire sprang up on one end.

"Gate's closed," Mark said. "Hang on."

The heavy Cadillac was still accelerating when it hit the electric iron gate at forty miles an hour. Mark had time only to see the guard diving out of the way; then the iron grill slammed up from the bottom as the lower supports gave way, pivoting on the top hinges. The black iron framework bounced upward, but only high enough to smash the windshield from side to side with a million jagged, splintering cracks as the Caddy surged on forward, cleared the scraping drag of the metal on its roof, and lunged into the street.

Mark whipped the wounded car to the left, careening around a corner, slowing then, driving without lights in the blackness, thanks to the two broken sealed beam units in the fender wells. He drove the six blocks to the spot they had left the rental car with no challenge.

Mark dropped two blue flint arrowheads on the seat of the Caddy to match the four he had left in the garage.

"Ah, it seems we should make a change in our transportation," Tony said, mimicking W.C. Fields. They got out of the battered Cadillac and into the rental. The Caddy driver, still tied, was dropped back into the Cadillac, then Mark drove for the Bolyston Motel.

"So?" Tony asked.

"Cocaine, Tony. The society, snobbery drug. The white casket is coming in by sea within three days."

"And we're going to stop it," Tony said.

Mark measured him, wondering how far he could count on this man. At last Mark nodded.

"But I'll stop them, Tony. This is my hassle, not yours."

"I bought in, Mark. It's my name they're using. And

111

the quicker we get this cleaned up, the sooner I see my family again. When I left three years ago, I was confused, angry, really mixed up. Now I'm not, Mark. Now I know that my wife and my son are the most important things in the world to me."

Mark's doubts eased. He could watch Tony and try him. The man had a lot at stake. The Penetrator could trust Tony for what was coming.

"Let's get back to that motel and have some sleep. We might have to bug out at any time on a run to catch the *Anna Two* and its white casket cargo."

Chapter Nine

TWO DOWN AND DEAD

The phone kept ringing. Mark heard it through a dank and thickly repressive fog. He was struggling against something he couldn't see, couldn't grasp, something that vanished in front of him. Then he blinked open his eyes, coming awake instantly, his hand reaching for the red decorator-type phone.

"Yeah?"

The soft laugh was almost a giggle. A woman.

"Mark, are you always such a bear when you wake up?"

Then he had the voice; the voice print tallied with his memory banks and he sighed.

"Only when spoiled little rich girls call me too early. What's the trouble, Angie?"

"No trouble; why does there have to be trouble? What's happening?"

"I *was* sleeping."

She laughed. "Poor baby. Alone, I hope. Hey . . . well, I got something to talk to you about. You know . . . about our current problem. Can you scoot over here right away?"

Mark checked his watch. "At six-thirty A.M.?"

"Sure, no traffic at all; we can talk. I've got this thing that's bothering me so I can't sleep."

"So talk now."

"Mark, I can't talk now, not on the damn phone!"

Her voice was different, with a touch of terror. Mark had heard it in other voices too many times before. "Okay, say half an hour. I'll be there."

"Right."

Mark hung up and looked at Tony. He had slept through it. At least his color was starting to come back now. The hunted, dazed look was fading from his eyes. Another two months and he'd be back to normal.

The Penetrator dressed quickly in dark slacks and a brown striped shirt, worn loose to cover his hardware. Angie had sounded scared. That could be bad. He took Ava and his Colt, then strapped on the wrist knife under his long shirt sleeve. The Penetrator took a look in his war chest, removed a full .45 magazine, and put it in his back pocket, then locked the double-safe aluminum bag and he was moving.

Mark circled the big hotel, parked at the rear, and went in the service entrance. He found the working man's elevator and took it to the seventh floor. The Penetrator moved quickly to the stairs and climbed

114

them quietly to the eighth floor, where he took a long, cautious look out the stairwell door down the carpeted hallway. He remembered where Angie's room was and stared at the closed door. The suite had only one entrance; he had seen that when he was there before. So they would be waiting for him. There was no way inside except right down the old gullet. If he were wrong, he'd apologize to Angie, kiss and make up.

But his mind told him there had to be somebody else in there, somebody waiting for him. His hyper-senses told him the same thing. It wasn't logic or actual physical perception; it was the old combat *feel*.

Mark saw no one else in the hallway. He went back down the stairs to the seventh floor, ran to the opposite staircase, and went up it as quietly as his Indian brothers walking on newly plowed ground. He paused as he saw a pair of black, polished shoes on the landing above him.

The Penetrator hugged the near wall, then moved on upward without a sound. Ava was in his left hand, leading the spiderlike crawl along the stairwell wall. He got all the way to the top of the steps and swung around the corner; the other man hadn't turned. The stranger had a carbine in his hands with a foot-long silencer on the barrel. Mark brought up the dart gun before he spoke.

"Waiting for someone?" Mark asked.

The man spun, disbelief on his face, the carbine and long silencer muzzle swinging awkwardly toward Mark, his eyes growing wide as his finger pulled the trigger before the weapon came on target. Ava spoke quietly, the dart thudding into the rifleman's belly, penetrating a shirt and tee shirt, blasting its load of tranquilizer and muscle-constricting agent deep into his flesh.

The finger on the trigger reacted once more; then all the man's muscles seemed to be jerking, trembling, and jolting into uncontrollable spasms and cramps. The weapon fell from the man's hands and the Mafia hit expert slumped to the floor. Mark checked him to be sure; he didn't want to mistake an undercover cop for a Mafia goon. But most undercover cops carry some kind of identification on them. The man's pockets were empty except for a five-dollar gold piece with two Italian words on the back—the Mafia I.D. card.

Mark tensed his right hand and slammed the side of it hard against the underside of the hoodlum's nose. The Penetrator felt the small bones in back of the nose crush, knew that deadly splinters of bone and cartilage were being driven backwards, slanting through pulpy areas and directly into the Mafioso's brain. The body trembled; then a strong gush of air flowed from the man's mouth and at the same time Mark smelled the stench of feces as the involuntary muscles quit working. That was one hoodlum who had shit his pants for the last time.

Mark watched out the door a moment, then moved into the hallway and slid along the wall as quietly as he would stalking David Red Eagle in the washes around the Stronghold in California. He pressed his ear against Angie's door, and silently swore at expensive hotels—you couldn't hear a thing through solid doors.

He drew Ava, slid out the pack of tranquilizer darts,

and replaced them with the deadly, red-tipped curarine darts. Then he knocked three times, paused, and hit the door three more times and jumped sideways. As soon as the Penetrator saw the doorknob begin to turn, he sprang ahead and rammed into the partition with his shoulder, hitting it three feet from the floor. The heavy panel jolted backward. He heard a shout of surprise and pain, but the door continued inward and he dove, hitting the carpet on his right shoulder, half rolling, his right hand holding the dart gun and his left wrapped around the big .45.

As he rolled over, the dart gun fired twice. A man had been sitting in a chair directly across from the door, a sawed-off shotgun in his hands. He died with a look of surprise on his face, his finger not even on the trigger.

The man had watched his captive answer the door and waited, confident that she would jump back as he had ordered her to do, to give him easy coverage of the target. Then Fred down the hall would drill this meddler twice, silently with the carbine, and it would be all over. But when the girl had been hit and thrown backward by the force of the door, he had been so stunned that he had watched her fall, not even glancing up to see the cause.

One of the darts hit his left arm, enough to kill him in six seconds, and the other one vanished through his right eye. He slumped backward in the chair, staring at the ceiling with one eye, the deadly shotgun lying across his chest where it had fallen.

Mark turned toward Angie. She lay on the floor five feet beyond the door.

"My God, what hit me, a two-hundred-ton dump truck?" She sat up, pushing hair out of her face, shaking her head.

Mark holstered his weapons, pushed the door closed, then hurried to her. Angie was still groggy.

"You hurt bad?" Mark asked.

She didn't answer. He sat beside her on the floor, put his arms around her, and kissed her forehead. "Hey, little angel, are you still with us?" He looked at her legs and arms but saw nothing distended, no limb bent at the wrong angle. No blood, no bad bumps on her head. He kissed her forehead again.

"Lower down, dummy," she said.

Mark pecked at her lips and when he came away her eyes opened. Tears were starting to show at the corners. She looked at the man in the chair.

"He won't hurt you," Mark said.

"The other one?" she asked, starting to tremble. He held her tighter.

"No, he won't bother us either."

The tears came then, and the sobs, but she didn't let them last long. She choked them off, wiping the wetness away with the back of her hand.

"Who is being tough now?" she asked him, then pointed at the man in the chair. "They pushed their way in during the night, said I'd have to call you, but not until they were ready. They acted like they had orders, knew just what to do and how to do it. They were going to kill you!"

Mark eased his arms away from her. He had to do something about the corpses. He patted her hand and went to the windows, but none of them would open. There was no laundry chute, no dumbwaiter. He checked the hall; it was empty.

Mark ran to the end of the hall to the freight elevator and pushed the call button. When the car arrived, he set a barrel-like ash tray from the hall between the automatically closing doors to keep them open. The Penetrator rushed back to Angie's room and hoisted the dead Mafia soldier over his shoulder and hurried with him to the freight elevator. Then the Penetrator punched the roof button on the indicator and stepped out, letting the doors close and the car go up with its burden. He ran to the near stairwell and found the second hoodlum where he had dropped. Mark checked the stairwell and found a neat rectangle of space downward between the flights of stairs, extending to the basement.

He heaved the body up to the rail, aimed carefully, and dropped it. The Mafia soldier didn't get to the basement, but he fell four flights before he hit the railing and smashed his head open on the sturdy pipe and cement construction.

Mark grabbed the carbine and ran back to where Angie was peeking out her door.

"Where is he?"

"Don't worry about it," he said, checking the chair where the man had died. He could find no traces of blood. He ran to the bathroom and picked up two towels. Mark threw one to Angie.

119

"Wipe off everything they touched where they could have left fingerprints. We're taking no chances of linking you to this. Everything!"

They worked for five minutes; then Mark went around planting his prints where they had just wiped. He had on a pair of the semi-permeable thin plastic gloves with built-up fingerprints that the professor had developed. He left new prints on every mission. Sometimes he used two or three different sets.

"Now you do the same; put some prints on so the room won't look like everything was cleaned off."

She did, then looked up. "Can we go now? I want to get out of this awful room."

"No; get packed."

"What?"

"Packed—you're moving out of here. If these goons used you to get at me here, they know more about us than we can afford. Come on, let's move it!"

A little before 8:30 that morning Mark checked Angie in at the Fenway Commonwealth Motor Hotel. She signed a cover name of Mae Jones, and they went to the room.

On the way over she had explained to him that she had made one phone call to one of her oldest friends, a girl she had been in school with.

The girl evidently had told someone who had known the information was valuable and sold it to the Family.

"I swear I'll never use the damn telephone again, Mark. I won't, I pledge it."

"They told you to call someone. Did they use my name?"

She shook her head. "No; they said I knew a man who had been giving them a lot of trouble. They described you right down to that black Indian hair of yours, and told me to call you. It was one of those damn offers you can't refuse."

Mark shrugged. "So they know we're here. They know a little more about us than I had figured. So we have to move faster now. I'll call Tony and get him out of that place; they probably traced the phone call or relayed the number."

Before he could reach for the phone, she touched his arm.

"Mark, couldn't that wait for a while?" She smiled and put her arms around him, leaning against his chest. Her kiss came burning on his cheek, then on his lips.

"Angie, we just don't have time right now." He kissed her and they sat down slowly on the soft bed. She stretched out on her back, looking up at him.

"Mark, I just wanted to say that I—"

He didn't let her finish. His mouth came over hers, her eyes closed, and she sighed.

Just then the telephone rang.

Mark let it rattle five times, then rolled away from Angie, and she grabbed it.

"Miss Jones, you asked to be called about a good place to rent a car. We believe you'll be more than satisfied with the Belmont Rental just down the block from us."

"Yes, that's good. Thank you," Angie said, and hung up.

Mark sat up, then stood. "Look, Angie. I better call

Tony and let him know where I've vanished to and that you've moved, right?"

Angie nodded, half smiling. "And if you don't hurry up and get back over here, *I'll* be trying to kill you!"

Mark moved to the phone, remembering the number of the Fenway Boylston Motel, then dialed. The operator seemed excited when she answered. She asked Mark to hold, then came back on the line twenty seconds later.

"Now, may I help you?"

"Yes; ring 708, please."

"Oh, no, I can't. We've had some trouble. That room and the one next to it were in some kind of an explosion about half an hour ago. I'm afraid the police and firemen are there and the phone is not working. Everything is just a mess. Maybe I can take a message. Some people got hurt pretty bad."

Mark dropped the phone and jumped off the bed, where he had sat down to call.

"Our room at the Boylston Motel just got bombed. You stay here." Mark ran out the door and down to the parking lot.

Chapter Ten

FOUR QUEENS AND A GOAT

Mark parked half a block from the motel and went toward it from the side. There were two fire trucks, half a dozen police cars, and a hundred people standing around the parking lot. The Penetrator studied the scene, not willing to walk into a situation where the law was waiting for him. Had the police opened his suitcase filled with weapons and explosives?

He scanned the gawking crowd, then spotted Tony walking back and forth behind a car halfway down the parking lot. Mark took long strides toward the slender man, who had his hands stuffed deep in the pockets of his blue jeans.

"*¿Que passo?*" Mark asked, and Tony turned, surprised at the Spanish phrase he hadn't heard since his days at UCLA. His eyes showed a touch of relief as he laughed nervously.

"Where the hell did you run off to? I've been trying to figure out what to do. I'm okay, but that room we had is a mess."

Mark explained his sudden trip and the threat against Angie. He motioned toward their former room, where the roof had fallen in.

"How did you get out of that?"

"I heard you just as you left, so I got up, trying to catch you. But by the time I had put on my pants and shirt, you were gunning out the driveway. So I had some coffee in the restaurant and decided to wait for you so we could talk things over. But you didn't come back. I had breakfast; then the damn bomb went off. It was outside the room next to ours, that's what the cops think. So most of the damage was in the next room."

"They worked fast," Mark said. "At least you weren't in there when it blew. Now how do we get our gear back?"

"Oh, I checked with the manager. He said the firemen took all the personal property out of both rooms. I went up and identified our gear and he supplied us with a new suitcase for one of mine that got bashed in. I told him we wouldn't sue him and he looked relieved. The guy in the other room got mashed up pretty bad, I guess. They took him away in an ambulance."

A half hour later they had moved their belongings to the Fenway Commonwealth Motel and taken another room near Angie's. Angie grinned when she saw Tony wasn't hurt.

"I knew nobody was gonna hurt my tough big

brother," she said, giving him a hug. She led him to the big, soft chair, and Mark marveled at how appealing she was, in so many ways.

Tony nodded. "So Big Mike is starting to hit back. That means we have to move faster, doesn't it, Mark? So when do we move in and get Monica and little Tony?"

"Damned soon, Tony. They should know that I'm the one hurting them by now. I've given them enough notice. I've been trouble for other Families before and they know me. So now they'll be gunning for me, and they won't wonder if you might have come back from the dead. That's a break."

Angie glanced up at him, curious, but said nothing.

"Tony, where would the Family handle uncut drugs? They'd need a kind of laboratory, a clean room, fine measuring and weighing instruments, some kind of packaging. Any idea?"

Tony had several, including a former wholesale drug firm the Family had always owned, and three more small business firms that he'd heard about but never knew what type of action went on there.

"Of course it all could have changed in the past three years, man. No reason it should have, but we can check," Tony said.

"Let's go take a look."

Angie jumped up. "Hey, no fair leaving me here with nothing to do. Haven't you guys heard about equality for women, about women's lib? What can I do?"

Mark watched her, saw the smile spread over her

beautiful face, and he thought she was the prettiest woman he had ever seen. He grinned and nodded. There were a thousand things he'd like to do with this girl walking beside him, places to travel, sights to see, evenings to spend, but he knew that would never be. He moved to the black suitcase, the one where they stashed the Mafia numbers bank money they had liberated. Inside were dozens of stacks of bills. He took a quarter-inch stack of twenty-dollar notes and handed it to the girl.

"Operating money. Go rent a car and drive out near the *Anna Two*," Mark said. "Find some place where you can stay without being obvious. Rent a room, find a restaurant, park your car, anything so you won't attract attention and can stay for about twelve hours. We want to know the moment the *Anna Two* leaves the dock. If she gets underway for any reason, get in touch with us here. Leave a message with the desk. For this operation we should have radios, but I've never needed them before. Anyway, keep tabs on that boat; it's the key to the whole white casket caper."

Angie nodded, intent on her instructions. "Yes, okay, I've got it, I've got it. I'll find a place out there. I know that area." She paused. "Hey, you two, now don't go and get in any trouble. I mean, I don't want either one of you hurt, y'hear?" She kissed her brother on the cheek, then kissed Mark on the lips and laughed as Tony groaned.

An hour later, Mark and Tony checked out the third store Tony had figured might be used for the drug-cutting work. It was a legitimate warehouse, with semis, bobtails, and lots of fork-lift trucks hustling around the loading docks. Inside were stacks and huddles of boxed goods.

"Let's try one more," Tony suggested. The address was in South Boston, a small, clean building on the corner with no doors in front, two high, small windows, and a sign that said simply: *South Boston Insurance*. Mark parked on the side street and opened the battered aluminum suitcase.

Everything inside seemed intact. He took out two pencil-type detonator-timers, which had been carefully packed in foam rubber to cushion them, and two rectangles of C-5 explosive, the advanced, just-developed charges that more than tripled the power of the old C-4.

"This one looks like it could be a winner," Mark said, stuffing the explosives in his back pockets and the detonators in his shirt. He slid an extra magazine of .45 ammo in his pocket and pushed the .45 in its clip-on belt holster just under the long shirt.

"Let's take a look at the back door," Tony said.

It was locked. Mark bent over the alley door, and a few seconds later had the lock open. He eased the panel forward a crack and looked inside, then edged it further ajar. Inside he saw a small back room, with a long, counter-type work table, two chairs, and a cot. Both men slid into the room with their weapons out. Mark moved on Indian-quiet feet to the doorway ahead. He listened at the panel, then turned the knob slowly. The door was not locked. It swung toward him, so Mark eased it open until he could see a sliver of the area beyond.

The Penetrator let out his breath, realizing he had been holding it since they had come through the outside door. It *was* a cutting operation. He had seen enough of them before to know—the expensive scales, clean table, workers in white smocks and wearing plastic gloves. Four women leaned over the tables or worked at the scales. Mark frowned. Something wasn't right. Was it a legitimate operation?

Then he saw the man at the end of the table. He had "hoodlum" written all over him. His coat was off and he wore a shoulder harness with a .38 hanging from it in a pressure holster. The gun butt hung downward for an easy draw.

Mark went through the door silently, and only when the man looked up and growled did Mark speak.

"Don't move, anyone!" Mark barked, his .45 Commander reinforcing the demand. He waited as Tony moved around the line of fire and picked the weapon from the man's dangle holster. The Mafia goon turned then and stared at Tony.

"Hey, what's going on? Why are *you* down here? What the hell's going on?" The big man stared at Tony a moment more, then looked back at Mark. "Oh, shit!" he exploded. "The damn maniac with the arrowheads. I saw you out in Los Angeles!"

Mark shot him once through the heart, the 200-grain Hensley and Gibbs slug blasting the life from him in a millisecond as the Mafia soldier jolted backward, only a slight indentation on his brown sports shirt where the messenger entered his chest. His eyes glazed, his knees folded, and he pitched forward on his face with a long, death-rattle sigh.

Two of the women screamed when the .45 roared. The other two held back tears and shock as they cowered against the rear wall.

Mark ran to the table and put a wet finger in the white powder, then tasted it. He turned toward the paralyzed quartet of women.

"Do any of you know what this is?"

"Some kind of expensive chemical, he told us," one woman said. She was older than the rest.

Another woman, the smallest of the group, with black eyes and long, black hair to match, looked up defiantly. "At least we're not cold-blooded killers. You're a murderer."

Mark brushed it aside. "Did he tell you this was illegal, this packaging work?"

"Yes, and that we shouldn't talk about it," the black-eyed one said. "But he told us it was nothing to be ashamed of."

"Ladies, this *is* something to be ashamed of. This is *heroin.*"

One of the women fainted. The others groaned. The girl with the black eyes leaned against the wall and tears ran down her cheeks.

"Mother of God! We didn't know, I swear it. I swear we didn't know it was that poison, that gmulch!"

Mark worked quickly then, and with Tony's help stacked the uncut heroin and the five cases of packaged goods next to it; then he fit the oblong block of clay explosive under the pile.

"Ladies, I want you to take your things and get out of here. Leave quickly and go home. If anyone asks you about this, just forget what we look like, or better, say you never saw us. It happened after you left. Your boss there was a Mafia hoodlum. He had no right to be living. Some of his Mafia friends might try to see you, so drop out of sight for a while; take a little vacation."

They nodded. Two left; the one who had passed out was slower getting to the door. The small girl with black hair was last. She paused and swallowed.

"Thank you for . . . for telling us." She looked at Mark, sighed. "I'm sorry I said bad things about you." Then she turned and ran out the door.

Mark placed the other charge against an interior support wall that would cause the most damage. The roof would blow off and the back walls fall inward. Then the second timed charge would blast the heroin into a billion grains of powder that no one would ever be able to recover. But the police would find plenty of evidence of the cutting operation. Mark left the dead Mafia soldier where he lay. He wouldn't mind being buried by a pile of wood.

Mark set the fuses on the timers, inserted them deep into the plastique C-5, and the men left by the back door. They drove two blocks away, where they could see the back of the building, and parked. The first muffled explosion came exactly on time. A few boards flew off the roof of the one-story building; then the rear

130

wall blew out and the rest of the building settled downward in a whooshing rush of dust.

A minute later the second blast came with a sharp, thunderous explosion, breaking nearby windows and pre-cutting half the building into kindling wood. Mark had left three arrowheads and was sure one would be found. It should put a little more pressure on Big Mike Sollozzo.

Tony turned to Mark. "Now is the time, buddy. Now we go and get Papa away from them." Tony paused. "Mark, I know you've been fighting against the Mafia for two years now. I know the whole story, about the arrowheads. I looked it all up in old issues of the newspaper. I understand how you feel. Papa is a Mafia Don and he's got blood on his hands, lots of it. You might think he deserves anything he gets. But, Mark, he's still my father, and I simply *have to help him*! If you don't want to go with me, fine; let me do it by myself!"

Chapter Eleven

ONE ROOM, NO WAITING

Mark studied the man sitting beside him. Tony rapped his fingers nervously on the seat, keyed up, intense, nearly angry. Mark knew old Don Carlo had dried blood up to his armpits, but he was Tony's father. Tony had been a real help so far. Hell, it was time to bend a little and return the favor.

"Okay, Tony. We'll go in and get him. But first we go back to our motel and see if we have any messages from Angie and then set up our strategy. I think I know where your father is, or at least where he was. All we can do is take a try at it. But we'll have to go in as soft as possible."

Tony relaxed; a nervous tic at his right eye faded away. "Good. Any way you want to do it, Mark, just so we get into action."

Mark checked the time, a little after noon. They

drove to the Fenway Motel but had no message from Angie. They caught a quick lunch and Mark read the Boston Globe.

A story splashed across the front page with a banner headline. *"Penetrator Attacks Boston!"* The story went on to report some of his recent exploits and how dozens of police jurisdictions were searching for him on a variety of charges. A composite picture ran on the front page but looked nothing like the tall, lean Indian. The Boston police bomb squad had found two arrowheads at the home of Carlo Rossi, reputed kingpin of the Boston Mafia. Similar arrowheads had been found at the scene of a killing, but police had kept the fact secret until they could investigate it further.

The reporter had done his homework, digging up more than a full page of editorial matter and pictures from files and wire dispatches about the Penetrator and his crusade against crime. Only in the paper it looked more like a one-man crime wave. This story did emphasize that the Penetrator aimed his attacks at all levels of criminals, and that some said he was a modern-day Robin Hood. Mark folded the paper and put it down.

Tony had been grinning as the big man read. He took a bite of his rare steak and pointed his knife at the story.

"How are the press reviews so far?" he asked softly.

Mark shrugged. "If it helps us shake up Big Mike, it's done its job. There's no sense having a trademark if it won't work for you. So far it's done well. If it works now it might confuse Big Mike enough so we can get in

134

and out with your father without endangering a bunch of civilians."

Tony nodded. "Good. I really don't like to use that .45 of mine." He chewed a bite of steak. "I mean, over there in Guinea in the jungles and swamps, I swore I'd never walk around *anywhere* again without a .45 if I could ever get my hands on one. Now it doesn't seem so important. Before this I've never had any need for a pistol. Now just to walk in and start blasting somebody . . ." His voice trailed off. "I don't like killing people, Mark."

"You'd make a lousy Mafia hit man, you know that?" Mark was silent for a moment. "Tony, I don't like doing some of the things I have to do. But sometimes that's the only way. It must be done and the courts and the police are too slow, too *unsure*. When I find scum who are bleeding poor people dry, who are on the killing end of big crime orders, I move in and do the job. These guys are living on borrowed time."

Mark stopped, lifted his dark brows. "Sorry, Tony, usually I don't give motivational dissertations this way."

"No sweat." Tony said. Then he frowned. "No sweat. We had a guy in school who said that, remember? 'No sweat' was about the only comment you could get out of him."

Mark remembered.

It took them two hours after lunch to set up the scam. First they rented a Ford panel Econoline truck at Econo-Car Truck Rental at 7 Eliot Street. Mark made sure it had no company logo on its side; it was a new rig not yet painted. At a nearby medical supply store they rented an ambulance-type gurney, a stretcher with folding wheels. Then they drove to Baxter Costume Company at 24 Lincoln Street off Sumner in back of Jordan Marsh. Mark was impressed by the sign that said the costume firm had been in business since 1872. After a short talk with a clerk they walked out with two pairs of coveralls that had *"Ace TV Repair"* logos on the backs.

By the time Tony and Mark drove to the Continental Gardens Sanitarium, it was after two-thirty. They circled the place, then parked across the street and Mark studied it. A high brick wall around what they could see on this side had wires on top with insulation, so they might be electrified. The front was posh, with a guard and a gate, but it was for looks only—it was nothing that could stop an Econoline van in a rush. Mark let it all fall into place in his computer, then wheeled up to the small guard post and skidded the wheels on the paving as he put on his mad-as-hell act.

"Goddamn, is this really the right place, Continental Gardens? Hell, we've been over half this end of town looking for you guys, you know that? We're half an hour late and we're gonna get ass chewed from the guys inside and the boss back at the office. Where is the goddam central lounge?"

The middle-aged guard, who had left the Boston police force two years before, leaned back as if struck. His face reddened and he stuttered as he replied. He'd seen enough trouble in his time not to cross this mean-looking sonofabitch.

"Middle door, building on the left," the guard said, then stepped back without another word.

Mark shook his head in disgust. He was still swearing a green stream of invectives at the guard, the gate, the day, the sanitarium, and his boss as he pulled away. The Econoline rolled past the barrier, up a short, curved drive, and stopped in front of the building the guard had indicated. It looked like the main door of the place. Mark turned the rig and headed it back toward the street, then looked over at Tony.

"Well, we're in, soft as hell."

Tony laughed, trying to hold back his surprise. "Hey, man, you could go on the stage. You're good."

Mark grabbed the tool kit the costume store had furnished them, to which he had made some special additions. Tony got out of the truck and headed for the front door.

Inside the heavy double doors, the thick carpet swallowed up their shoes as they walked to a reception table and a pretty girl with a long, slender face.

"Hey, we're supposed to fix the TV set in the boss man's office," Mark said. "President or director or some damn title."

The girl's frozen smile almost cracked, her green eyes appraising Mark openly.

Mark watched two six-foot orderlies go by in hospital blue operating gowns. One jangled keys and opened a door, then went out of the lobby.

"I'll call Mr. Duncan," she said, her voice interestingly low.

"He knows we're comin' and we're late and he's

gonna be mad as hell. Just take us in there and save some time."

She looked at Mark again, smiled faintly and stood, leading them the opposite way the orderlies had gone and through an unlocked door.

The hallway here was just as posh, with deep shag carpeting and oil paintings on the walls. When she opened the office door, there was more of the same in a twenty-foot-square office with a wet bar against one side and an eight-foot picture window. The receptionist closed the door and retreated.

"We're here about your TV set that went on the blink," Tony said. "Some woman called us."

The man behind the desk rose from a six-hundred-dollar executive leather swivel rocker that matched perfectly the shade of teakwood in his free-form desk. His face was at once alert, curious. Mark jumped forward, catching the man's arm, and then pressed his fingers against the stranger's carefully shaven and lotioned throat. One finger stabbed into a nerve, making the director's vision blur and his knees go rubbery, so he slumped into the chair.

"What is this?" he demanded, his voice weak.

"Information, Mr. Duncan," Mark said, reading from the desk name plate. "You have a patient here, Carlo Rossi. We've come for him."

Mark eased his finger pressure.

Duncan blinked twice, then looked at Tony. "Mr. Rossi is an extremely sick man. He is in the final stages of lung cancer and there is nothing we can do for him. It's inoperable and can't be touched with chemotherapy

138

or radio-therapy. To move him right now could kill him."

"We'll take that chance," Tony said at once. "We both have guns and can use them. We *will* use them, Mr. Duncan, unless you do exactly what we say. Is your life worth protecting Don Carlo any more?"

Weakly the man shook his head.

"Then take us to him at once," Mark said. "Don't signal or indicate anything is wrong. Bring any keys you'll need for the doors. Remember, one false motion and you're as good as turkey meat."

Duncan reacted to the term, and Mark knew he was deeper into the Boston Mafia scene than it seemed. Duncan shivered when Mark released him. A quick pat-down turned up a small .22 Derringer in his suit pocket. Mark took it and motioned the man to the door. A small portable TV sat on the edge of the big desk. Mark pointed at it, and Tony pulled the plug and carried it with them, following Mark.

The small caravan went out the door, made two turns in the carpeted hall, and then down a second long hallway, stopping in front of a door. Duncan hesitated, then stepped up and slid the door back into the frame and moved inside. The other two followed him. A form lay on a hospital bed. The figure faced the wall and was covered with a blanket. Tony ran to the bed, took a big breath, and then touched the blanket. At his touch Tony screamed and jolted backward. Mark's reaction was nearly fast enough as he lunged for the door, trying to get his steel-capped boot toe between the closing electronic panel and the wall. But it slammed shut. Tony had been thrown six feet from the bed and now slumped on the floor holding his burned hand, a shocked, dazed expression on his face.

Mark knew it was useless to try the door. He examined the rest of the room in a twentieth of a second: no outside window, no grates or ducts entering the room except a small one at the ceiling where a recessed light bulb hung. No other doors or panels leading from the room. It was a death cell. The shape on the bed was not a body, but a long lump of blanket with a high electrical charge.

The voice came almost at once.

"Well, so you finally came. We're not sure who you are, but we're delighted you're here. You won't be for long, though. This room is hermetically sealed, and the hissing you will soon hear is a deadly nerve gas which will completely fill the room in thirty seconds. . . ."

Mark tried not to listen. He jerked open the tool bag he still carried and took out a small square of the old C-4 explosive. It was a quarter pound. He plastered it against the latching side of the electric door. Another three seconds passed, and he pulled out the electric fuse and jammed the detonator into the C-4, then spread the leads. He had used seven seconds.

"Get down on the floor near this wall," Mark shouted over the other voice. "Hands over your ears, mouth open. Don't breathe," he ordered.

"We hadn't planned on having your company so soon, and if you are the Penetrator, I'll be more than pleased. The bounty on your head is up to half a million dollars now, Mr. Penetrator. It was thoughtful of you to stop by. I think I'd better turn on the gas now. Pleasant dreams!"

The gas began hissing into the room.

Mark pulled out the small battery-powered pack to furnish the spark to set off the explosive. Furiously he wrapped one wire around a lead, then the second one. He took a shallow breath, smelled nothing, leaned against the wall, and closed the plunger. The world ended.

The blistering shock wave slammed Mark six feet sideways, smashing him against the wall with what felt like an atom blast force. His ears split open and seemed to disintegrate in continuing clanging cymbals in the small room. Mark felt his lungs drained of every particle of air as they were sucked dry by the grasping concussion of the blast; then the thin, deep snarl of the explosion reached his ears, bursting his eardrums, he was sure. A quarter of a pound of C-4 in a room that size was suicide, but so was waiting for the goddamned gas!

Mark felt blood in his nose, blood on his lips. He tried to roll over, but found Tony draped over him. The man was on his knees now, trying to crawl.

Mark sat up, the terrible pain yammering at him, punching through his defenses, drilling into his brain, setting his whole nervous system on fire in one massive, shocking wave of pain, agony a millionfold all compressed into one millisecond of life. His eyes cleared, blurred, cleared again. The door was gone, blown into the hall. The smooth voice from the grate above was stilled. Mark heard nothing, no sound. He lifted his arm experimentally. Not broken. He moved his other arm, then each leg, and all were intact. But his head kept pounding, screaming at him, pleading for mercy from the hellish pain as if he were being lowered slowly into a crucible of molten steel.

Tony stood, swayed, drew his .45, and staggered to the door opening, expecting to see a score of curious faces in the hall. Only one person was there, Duncan, crumpled against the far wall. The hallway was empty, but pictures had been blown off the walls. A cart filled with linens had tipped over, its load scattered down the hallway.

Mark checked nearby rooms. All the rooms were empty; no one had been there for some time. He struggled back to the death pit and looked at Duncan. He hadn't tried to speak yet. Mark's mouth was dry, his lips like crocus cloth, his throat one deep, parched tunnel.

"Alive?" Mark asked Tony, pointing to Duncan. Tony didn't hear the word. Mark scowled. He hadn't heard it either. Had he spoken? He had. He touched Tony's shoulder, gave him a thumbs-up sign, and Tony nodded.

Mark knelt in front of Duncan. He tried to talk again, but his words made no contact, even with his own ears. Mark touched the man, and using signs and motions, got across the point that he wanted him to take them to Rossi.

Duncan shook his head. He held his left arm carefully with his right. Mark slapped the broken arm and saw Duncan's mouth open in what must have been a scream of pain. Mark and Tony pulled the man to his feet and propelled him to the door. Mark pointed one way. Duncan shook his head. They turned in the direction they had been going. Now hatred mixed with pain and fury marred Duncan's face.

They went through another door, down a short hall, and Mark again wondered where the other people were, the curious, the patients. Then he remembered he had seen no other patients. None. Was there only one? Duncan led them to another door and stopped.

Inside the room a woman in a nurse's uniform sat reading. A soap opera played on a big TV set. An old man, shrunken, distorted, eyes watering, his breath coming in wheezing gasps, lay on the bed. He had no tubes or wires fastened to him; no heroic measures were being taken to prolong his life.

Tony ran to the bed, looked at the man, turned, and nodded to Mark. He touched the blanket tentatively, then firmly, and found no electrical charge. Duncan collapsed into a second chair. The nurse sat petrified, looking straight ahead. Tony pulled a sheet around the hundred pounds of shrunken flesh and soft bones and lifted Don Carlo Rossi in his arms. The old eyes did not understand; the voice did not speak.

Mark lifted Duncan and pushed him ahead as he led them out of the room and to the front door of Building Five. The Penetrator saw only the receptionist in the lobby. Outside, they had Carlo Rossi firmly strapped to the gurney in the panel truck when Mark saw the men coming.

Mark shouted something, but knew Tony couldn't

hear him. He hit Tony's shoulder, pointed out the drive several times with his finger, and drew his .45. He slammed the back door and Tony started the engine.

The Penetrator dove behind a low stone wall and fired twice at the pair of "orderlies" he had seen before, who came around the end of the building. One had a handgun, the other an M-16. Mark used up one clip, keeping the men pinned down behind the wall, until he saw Tony smash through the gate. Rossi was away and safe.

The big Indian crawled the length of the wall, then sprinted for the near corner of the next building and saw dust fly as two rounds hit near his feet. Then he was around the structure, looking at the high brick wall at the rear of the estatelike sanitarium.

Mark darted behind a thick tree next to the wall and crouched, then saw two more men come from the opposite side. One had an M-16, and he lifted it and let loose a stuttering trail of lead into the trees around Mark.

The Penetrator watched the four men for a moment. None could see him, but all knew generally where he was. He decided they wouldn't risk too much use of the M-16's; that would attract attention, even in Boston. The men moved in quick infantry-type surges from one spot of cover to the next. These guys knew what they were doing.

Another swatch of hot, angry lead from the .223 bore chewed holes through the branches over Mark's head. He looked at the wall, then back at his attackers.

Chapter Twelve

BOARDERS AWAY!

Mark took a small concussion grenade from his pocket. It was about a third the size of a standard grenade and exploded with a great noise but a minimum of shrapnel. He pulled the pin and threw it well beyond the closest attackers. Then he stepped to the brick wall and began working his way up the vertical surface. His fingers and toes found depressions most people wouldn't notice. When the grenade went off he felt the concussion but heard nothing.

He kept crawling higher, higher. Mark saw one man start toward his position, then veer away. Mark lifted himself again, then felt his fingers edge over the top of the wall. He kept moving, working upward with his feet, pivoting his body, until his legs were nearly the same height as his head. Then he rolled onto the flat top of the brick wall, sharing the space with the wires he was sure were electrified.

He lay perfectly still as one of the hunters ran into the area below, where Mark had been. If the gunman had looked up, he would have seen Mark. But he didn't; he only swore, checked the soft ground for footprints, then ran along the trail. Mark eased his feet under him and came to a crouching position, stepped over the three strands of wire, and jumped to the ground on the far side of the wall.

Forty-five minutes later Mark had hailed a taxicab and ridden to the motel and approached the rented Econoline with caution. It had taken him a dozen tries to give the cab driver his destination. His ears still weren't right. He couldn't hear the driver at first. But as the ride continued, he began to hear the first faint sounds of traffic, then a horn, and Mark smiled. When the cab driver told him the fare was two-fifty, Mark paid it gladly because he had heard him almost normally.

Mark checked the Econoline, but found no one there, so he ran across the motel parking lot to the room at the Fenway Commonwealth. Tony was at the door, giving instructions to a sturdy, efficient-looking nurse. The old man lay on the big bed.

Tony waved Mark outside.

"Your ears working yet?"

"Fair, but don't start yelling," Mark said.

"Angie called. She says there's action down at the *Anna Two*. This may be the day. I told Angie to charter a boat that would do at least fifteen knots so we can catch them if they take off before we get there."

Mark rubbed his ears without realizing it. They still hurt; he didn't know if his inner ear was damaged or not. He asked Tony to get the aluminum case containing his weapons from the room, which he did.

"Come down when you're ready to roll. We should be getting over to where Angie is."

Tony nodded.

Down in the parking lot, Mark opened the bag in the van and took out two loaded magazines for his Commander, stuffed fresh loads in the dart gun, and did some tall thinking. At a nearby telephone booth he made four calls. On the fifth one he made the contact he needed, and he let a small smile shift across his features.

Tony came toward the Econoline and Mark laid it out for him.

"I've got to make a stop on the way to the *Anna Two*. There's no way I can get you inside this place I'm going, so you take the other car and I'll meet you at Angie's lookout as soon as I can."

Tony didn't ask any questions, which pleased Mark. They parted and Mark said he'd be there within an hour.

As it turned out, Mark arrived only half an hour after Tony did. Mark's new purchases were wrapped in heavy brown paper and in an unmarked box. Again Tony didn't ask any questions.

Angie had parked next to a small restaurant and had a perfect view of the slip where the *Anna Two* lay at anchor. She slid over as Mark got into the front seat of the car.

"I hear you guys have been busy," she said. "Tony says Daddy looks bad, but we're going to be with him for just as long as we can, as long as he lasts, right after this is all over."

Half-dried tears made tracks down her pretty cheeks. She smiled. "Thank you, Mark. I know it was hard for you." She leaned over and kissed his lips, then settled back. "Now to business. I saw six men go on board. Three had on good clothes, and three looked like crew, stocking caps and all. They took on some kind of cargo from a pickup truck. I couldn't see what it was, some brown cardboard boxes and paper sacks. They started the diesel engines about half an hour ago and idled them for a while. Now I think they're shut down. Looks like they're waiting for something, maybe the clock."

She pointed below to another slip, out of sight of the bigger boat. The little marina boasted a three-color sign. "I've got a twenty-five-foot Chris Craft rented down there. It has a small cabin, bunks for four, and will do thirty knots. I gave him three hundred deposit and he's getting it ready. I told him I wanted it for fishing."

They locked Angie's car and drove the Econoline down to the boat rental agency. It took them five minutes to load their gear on board. Tony walked to the top of the small rise where he could watch the *Anna Two.*

Mark started the engine. It ran smooth and steady,

and had more power than he expected. This Chris Craft would work just fine as a chase boat. He was still warming up the engine when Tony came down the slope and said the *Anna Two* had just cast off from the dock.

Mark gave Angie the wheel and the sleek little sportster got underway. Mark wanted to be sure she could handle it alone. As it turned out, Angie was an expert with small boats. She turned upstream and soon met the *Anna Two*. Both men were out of sight in the cabin and Angie wore big sunglasses. She continued upstream for a few hundred yards, then turned and trailed the larger ship down the Charles River.

The Penetrator willed himself to relax. The girl could handle the boat as well as he could. She watched the channel and passed the larger fisher at the widest spot in the river as they worked downstream out of the Charles and into the old harbor, then out past Logan International Airport. She took it easy, keeping half a mile ahead of the *Anna*. Just past Fort Independence, Angie turned the boat to the right and slowly made her way around Spectacle Island, letting the larger craft move ahead out past the lighthouse and seaward of Gallups Island. Then Angie turned on more speed and moved parallel to the other boat.

"Get ahead of her about a mile farther out," Mark said. "Then come around and go dead in the water so you can hail her for help."

Angie said she would, then slipped out of her blouse and skirt. She wore a skimpy halter and short shorts. "This might help to get their attention," she said.

149

Mark had been working over his new toy in the covered cabin. He made a small adjustment, then fit the two long, pipelike sections together and smiled.

Five minutes later the smaller boat lay dead in the slight Atlantic chop and the *Anna Two* steamed toward her, only fifty yards off the course. Angie, with big sunglasses and her brief outfit, stood on the sharp bow of the craft, waving an orange scarf.

The larger boat held course but slowed. As it came closer three men came to the bow rail and stared at her. One had field glasses.

"Help!" Angie screeched.

The larger craft's engine cut off. It turned closer and straightened out thirty feet away as the two boats bobbed in the growing seas.

"Help me!" Angie called. "I can't get the damn engine to run," she yelled.

"Stand by, we'll move in closer, and get you started," the oldest of the three said. "Looks like some weather coming up."

Angie waved and got back to the cabin.

Mark and Tony waited out of sight in the cabin as the boats scraped together. One man timed the swells perfectly, stepped off the big boat to the Chris Craft's bow, and walked back to the cabin. As soon as he ducked inside out of sight, Mark shot him with a tranquilizer dart and tied him up. The Penetrator looked out the cabin window at the larger ship. As soon as he had an opening, Mark shot four times with the dart gun at the three men leaning on the rail. He hit two of them, and the third swore and ran. Tony scrambled out of the cabin and up to the larger ship, a 12-gauge shotgun in his hands. Before Mark got to the rail he heard the boom of the shotgun from above.

Tony was on the bridge before Mark finished tying the two unconscious men at the forward rail. He dragged them back by the bait tank where they wouldn't roll overboard, and stepped over the bloody remains of a crewman who had been almost cut in half by a shotgun blast of double-ought shot. Mark ran below to make a quick survey of the four staterooms.

In one a woman lay naked on a bunk, sipping a drink. She grinned in surprise when Mark kicked open the door. Mark jerked the door closed and locked it from the outside, then continued his sweep. He found one naked man, half-drunk, in the biggest cabin, trying to load a .45 magazine.

Mark's shot from his Commander spun the other .45 off the small table. The Penetrator's ears thundered from the sound of the weapon in the all-metal cabin, but he beat down the pain with total concentration.

"You have a name?"

"Yeah, dumbass, what's it to you?"

"Your life, if you're lucky."

He was a big man, six-three. Mark snorted. "Big Mike Sollozzo, you don't look so damn big now."

The man's head jerked upward, his eyes vicious with hatred. He stared hard at Mark, then looked away.

"Let me get my fuckin' pants on."

"No. On your feet and topside. Move it, fatso!"

It was true. Mike carried forty pounds more than he should. He glared as Mark prodded him up the stairs to the deck. The boat continued on its course, and Mark saw Angie heading the twenty-five-footer back toward the mainland as they had planned. Tony was encouraging the boat captain to follow the orders Big Mike had given him before settling down with his lady friend. The booming shotgun probably had shaken Big Mike out of his lovemaking and sent him scrambling for his weapon.

Topside, Mark sat Sollozzo on a bench next to the little galley vent and brought over the two men, who had not yet returned to consciousness.

"Sollozzo, we know all about the white casket. We know you're on your way to pick it up and that we stay on this heading until we are contacted by the trawler. Anything more you want to tell us?"

"Fuck you!"

Mark checked the other men, who were starting to move in their bindings. Both were tied with thirty-pound monofilament fishing line. One man was strictly soldier material. The other one was older, maybe a minor cog in the machinery, but that could wait. He tied Mike, making sure he was fast to the iron pipe behind the bench, then went to the bridge.

Mark didn't know the captain. He was not the same man who had piloted Mark on the *Anna Two* before.

"Is he giving you any trouble, my friend?"

Tony shook his head. "Our buddy here knows where to go, what to do, and how to stay alive. Sollozzo didn't want to be bothered during his recreation. We stay on this heading for about ten miles until we find a trawler. They send a small boat over and we return a man to their boat as security. They bring over the casket, we examine it, then if it's all in order, we give them the suitcase of cash and they go back, return our man, and we head for home."

"A hostage. They want a damn hostage," Mark said. "That's been a pattern of warfare and bargaining for over ten thousand years." He shrugged; he was stuck with it. The Penetrator glanced down at his boot. What would keep the hostage from spilling his guts the minute he was away from the ship? Unless Tony went, but then the hostage couldn't be sacrificed in order to get the dope and save the cash. He glanced at the compartment on his boot again. He'd heard it would work. It was worth a try. If it went the way Mark thought, the ship they contacted would be Mexican, and perhaps no one on board could speak or write English. It was the best hope he had left.

Mark went down the steps and checked his three prisoners. He took two of them below and locked them in one of the cabins. He dragged Sollozzo down the steps and threw him into the last cabin, his hands tied. Mark unlocked the woman's cabin and looked in. She was still naked, sitting crosslegged on a bunk playing blackjack.

"Look, Mack, I'm bought and paid for, and I get the cash, whether you guys want the action or not, dig? None of this no-screw, no-pay jazz. So come on in and enjoy. Hell, I'm not particular, not at my age."

"Lady, I've never been that hard up," Mark said and slammed the door as she threw a magazine at him.

Back on deck, Mark watched the water. They were

halfway out; in another hour they would be almost there. Plenty of daylight left. He double-checked everything, looked over the new toy he had picked up at the Boston underground arms store, and checked the load. It was all set. He leaned back, ready and waiting.

They saw her from a mile away. The trawler was a little over a hundred feet long, dead in the water. If she had a radio on the *Anna Two*'s frequency, she wasn't transmitting.

They pulled to within a hundred yards of the ship and waited. As soon as they turned off their power, a small boat put out from the trawler, the outboard motor sputtering. Mark ran below and untied the feet of the Mafia soldier prisoner, sat him up, and then took out the hypodermic needle from his boot case. The needle was loaded with novocaine. Mark felt for the right spot on the hoodlum's throat. He found the depression between the collar bones and put the needle in there, slanting it upward into the man's larynx. The two cubic centimeters of novocaine should turn off the Mafia soldier's voice for at least a half hour. Mark told the man what he had done, and that if he tried to talk it could injure his voice permanently.

"Buster, you do exactly what I tell you and I'll fix you up. We'll go topside; you get in a small boat and go over to this Mexican trawler. Don't say a word, just sit there, then we'll get you back. Understand?" The mafia soldier nodded. He tried to talk, but nothing came out. Mark led him on deck.

The small white boat from the trawler bobbed alongside and Mark helped the soldier into it.

Ten minutes later Mark spotted the painter coming back, this time with a large packing crate balanced on it, almost as big as the boat itself. The captain came down from the bridge and used the power winch and boom to lift the casket onto the deck. Then the small Mexican man jumped on board, holding a pistol, and motioned to see the money. Mark opened the suitcase, which was filled with neat stacks of hundred-dollar bills.

"There you are, my friend," Mark said. *"¿Dinero,* every dollar, just as we planned, *es verdad?"*

The man looked up, probably not understanding the English, but he could count. He put down the pistol and began checking the stacks, counted one, and kept working. That was when Mark hit him from behind with the butt of the Colt Commander. He slumped to the deck. The crewman holding the outboard to the *Anna Two* shouted and reached for a rifle. Tony's shotgun blast swept the foreign crewman out of the painter and into the cold Atlantic.

Rifle shots popped from the trawler. Everyone took cover, and Mark threw the Mexican bandit into the sea, then grabbed the 3.5-inch bazooka from beside the bait tank and checked the load. He fastened the trigger wire, and lay on the deck where he had planned to, with the front of the tube through the rail and the rear aimed across an open space of deck behind him. Mark set the range, aimed, and fired.

The whooshing roar of the bazooka shrouded the

155

Anna Two with sound and haze for a moment, and the backblast scorched a *V* across the deck behind Mark. He tried to follow the flight of the rocket, but lost it, then saw it hit the side of the trawler above the water line and burst into an orange-red ball of fire, flame, and exploding steel.

The rifle fire stopped at once.

Mark grabbed another shell from the box and loaded it, wrapped the firing wire, and adjusted his sight. At this range he couldn't miss. He lifted his arm slightly and fired. The second round went over the rail into the superstructure and vanished before it exploded, then went off with a muffled roar.

"Crank it up!" Mark yelled at Tony, who hustled the captain back on the bridge.

Mark had time to get off one more shot at the trawler before the *Anna Two* began to move. The round hit near the stern and blew a pile of nets into useless string. Mark saw a small fire burning midships on the big craft.

"You'll never deal in junk again, I bet," Mark said. He turned and surveyed the haul: a hundred thousand in cash and a white casket loaded, he was sure, with enough cocaine or heroin to cause a million miseries, a hundred murders, and fifty suicides. Just then he heard Tony's cry.

"Mark, over here, I've been hit."

Chapter Thirteen

NOTHING PERSONAL

Mark ran to the stairs leading to the bridge and found Tony sitting on the top step holding his thigh. There was no blood. Using his Buck knife, Mark sliced open the pants over the small, round hole in the cloth. They found a crimson indentation starting to turn purple. The slug hadn't penetrated the back or side of his leg.

"Small," Mark said. "Probably a .22 or a .25 caliber. It wasn't a .223 from an M-16 or your leg would be half shot off."

"I didn't even feel it until I started climbing the stairs," Tony said. "Now it hurts like hell."

"I'll get the first-aid kit."

"Later, Mark. First bring Big Mike on deck."

Mark looked at him.

"Just bring up the sonofabitch and stay out of it, Mark."

"Personal?"

"You would say that in the army, I guess. But we say that there is really nothing personal about it. It's just business."

Mark frowned at the look in Tony's eyes as he said it. He had some idea what was coming as he pulled Sollozzo out of the cabin.

"What the hell's been going on? Sounded like a damn war up there."

Mark didn't reply. He left Sollozzo's hands tied and prodded him up the stairs to the deck. Big Mike was still naked. He shivered in the slight breeze.

"Shit, let me get some clothes on." He cocked his head when he saw that the request brought no response. "You really this Penetrator bastard I keep hearing about?"

Tony came from the side. He had a three-foot-long 2 x 4 that kept the live bait tank drain open. He swung it viciously, aimed over Sollozzo's waist, just in back of his side at his left kidney. The wooden club hit with a whack that blasted all pretense of normalcy out of the Mafia wheel. He shrieked in pain and terror, stumbled ahead, and kept his feet just long enough for Tony to crash the club against his other kidney. Sollozzo folded to the deck, vomiting a great, bilish green pool. He retched six times, then stared at Tony.

"Jesus! Jesus Christ! What's going on?"

Tony knelt in front of the screaming man, a fish filleting knife in his hand, the point scratching Big Mike's chin.

"Tony? What the hell you doing . . ." His words trailed off. "Hey, you don't look just right. I mean, God, we did a better match job than that. And we had . . ." He stopped, terror flooding his face, bulging his eyes, his hands moving toward the knife, then stopping.

"Sweet Christ . . . No. It can't be! Those damn headhunters killed you two years ago. No way!" He stared at Tony again. "Mother of God . . . is that really you, Tony? The real Tony Rossi? Tony, I been holding the Family together for you, ever since the old Don got sick. It's all yours, Tony, we been waiting for you!"

"Liar!" Tony screamed. He grabbed the man's tied hands and before Sollozzo could react, Tony had filleted the flesh off his first finger from palm to fingertip. Big Mike roared, stared in disbelief at Tony, then fell to the deck unconscious.

Tony turned on a two-inch wash-down hose and played a stream of cold sea water on the naked body until Big Mike came to.

Tony kicked him in the stomach and told him to sit up, then held the knife in front of him again, but this time he sliced the monofilament that bound his hands.

"Sollozzo, have you ever had life bad, I mean rotten, degrading, disgusting, painful, intolerable—so damn bad you wished to hell you *would* die? But somehow you live through that, and escape and overcome and get home—only to find that someone you trusted had taken over your house, your business, taken all of your

159

money and property, stolen your wife and family, and worst of all, hijacked *your face and your name!* No, Sollozzo, you'll never even begin to think what it could be like. It has to happen to you. You have to be there. Oh, sure, you saved the Family business for me. That's not what the soldiers say, Sollozzo. They say you're the *capo*, you're the boss man."

Sollozzo could barely speak. He looked up from the deck pleadingly. His words came slowly, carefully chosen.

"Tony. State Department, your tour sponsor, everyone said you had to be dead. Nobody survives down there, disease, snakes, and them damn savages, them cannibals. Nobody makes it out. Then your dad got sick, real sick; he couldn't move or talk. We hadda do something, so we put this together. It was just till you got back. When you came, great. If you didn't come, who got hurt?"

"Monica got hurt; little Tony got hurt!"

"We explained it all to her; she understands."

Tony's fist lashed out, hitting Big Mike on the cheek, toppling him on his side. He pushed back to his knees and Tony hit him a dozen more times, slugging him with angry hands, but with no real punishing effect. Tony began wincing each time a fist landed on the puffy face. He paused, arm tired.

"Sollozzo, you know me. You know I don't want the damn Mafia connections, the Family business. All I want is my own family, my wife and kid, and then I want to get out of this damn town." Tony grabbed Mike by each ear and pulled his head toward him.

"Were you going to trap me and keep me a prisoner if I ever did come back? Or was there a price on my head, a contract out?"

"No, Tony. No, nothing like that, I swear, we was hoping you'd get home."

Tony held the man's ears. "Mike, I had some primitive jailers for the past three years. When they caught a prisoner lying to them, guess what they did?"

"No, Tony, I'm not lying. Honest to God! I'll swear to you on my mother's grave!"

Tony moved his right hand forward from the ear until it touched Sollozzo's brow, then, with a slow, steady pressure the thumb dropped over the hard ridge into the depression of the eye socket. A quick, hard thumb gouge inward and Sollozzo's left eyeball tore from its socket, drooping on his cheek, held there only by a few white strings and cords with touches of blood on them.

Big Mike's roar of pain turned into a shriek before he passed out.

Tony stared at the result of his torture and pulled his hands away, letting the man flop on the deck. He thought of the hose, but leaned against the bait tank, panting, sobbing. He stared at the wreck of a man in front of him and his foot lashed out, kicking one leg.

Damn him! Right there was the cause of all of his pain and misery. Now it was pay-off time. Tony grabbed the hose, turned it on, and sprayed the helpless man again. Gradually the cold water shocked him back to consciousness.

With feeling came a howl of pain and horror. Sollozzo vomited, then held his head to try to deaden the terrible pain. His good eye remained closed.

"Stand up, Sollozzo. Stand up like a man. Are you a man or a sniveling dog in the gutter? Stand up like a Cosa Nostra soldier!"

Tony had heard the old Mafia rally cry often enough at parties and brawls and friendly fights. From some hidden reserve the Mafia soldier found strength to get to his knees, then stood, his good eye riveted on the mast holding the radio antenna.

"What's your name!"

"Mike Sollozzo."

"What's your Family?"

"Don Rossi, Boston."

"What's your position?"

"Third in command."

"Are you ready to die for the Family?"

"Yes; Family Before All!"

As he heard the ritualistic words, Tony lunged forward, the eight-inch knife daggering into Big Mike's belly to the hilt. Sollozzo's right eye looked down, his hands tried to hold the wound, but Tony pulled the scalpel-sharp blade upward, slicing through the small intestines, the descending colon, the iliac artery, and aorta before it bisected the right kidney and ripped into his stomach.

Tony jerked the blade free and watched the man fall, blood gushing from the eight-inch-long slash, splattering on the varnished wooden deck, running into the scuppers.

Big Mike's eye reached for Mark, who turned away, then for Tony.

"Nothing personal, Tony," the hoodlum said, spitting blood. Then he smiled.

Tony screamed, drew his .45, and blasted seven heavy slugs into Sollozzo's skull.

Tony stared at the battered, violated remains of the man, looked down at his .45; then his hand sagged. He turned away, screamed, and threw the big automatic as far as he could into the blue-green Atlantic.

"You've made me just as bad as you were!" Tony shouted, staring at the Mafia hardman. "I won't do it! I won't be like you were!"

Tony slumped to the deck halfway to the bow and stared out to sea for five minutes before he realized the ship was drifting. The motors were idling and the current moved them slowly.

Mark came and sat down beside him.

"How's the leg?"

"I'll live."

"I've been talking to the prisoner below. He's one of Sollozzo's command men down the line somewhere. Pure Mafioso. Shall I bring him up on deck?"

Tony waved. "Whatever you want to do, Mark. I'm through. I'll never hold a weapon in my hand again, *any kind* of a weapon. I won't even spank my kid. Maybe I'll be a librarian."

Mark touched his shoulder, went below, and brought up the older man who had been tied up. He left the crewman tied in his quarters. Mark cut the man's bonds and led him over so he could look at Mike Sollozzo's body.

"You ready for some of that?" Mark asked.

The small man's head shook.

"You have two choices: that, or a long swim. We're about five miles out; you probably won't make it."

The small man never hesitated. He kicked off his shoes and dove over the side. Tony watched him hit the water, surface, and stare back at him. Tony sighed, reached for a life preserver, and sailed it out to the man.

"Wind it up, Captain," Mark called, and the *Anna Two* began moving again.

It took them an hour to rip up the big packing box that held the white casket and then tear apart the box itself. Inside the lining they found a fortune in cocaine and heroin. All of it was dumped overboard, stripped from its plastic packages so it would dissolve in the sea.

Mark heard the woman pounding on her locked cabin door, but he ignored her. He cleaned up the evidence, throwing the shotgun overboard, along with the 3.5 bazooka and the three extra shells. He left big Mike where he lay. It would make a good story for the newspapers. But Mark didn't leave any arrowheads on board. No sense making things too easy for the police.

They were a mile off Gallups Island when they saw a sleek little power boat rushing toward them. It was the Chris Craft. Angie circled them once and they cut power. She waved that she was fine, then edged her boat against the bigger craft.

"Stay there," Tony told her. "We'll come aboard."

Before they left the *Anna Two*, Tony threw the ignition keys overboard. Mark cut the ignition wires and ripped out the radio.

He had a talk with the captain.

"You have a choice, Captain. Forget everything you saw or heard here, or be chopped up by the Mafia. Tell the Coast Guard you were tied up and left up here and saw nothing. You heard the shooting, but you don't know what happened. Understand?"

The captain agreed.

Mark tied him on the cabin floor, then put an old tee shirt around his eyes and tied it securely.

"Remember, you saw nothing, especially my buddy and me. You talk and I'll come back and hunt you down."

The captain nodded.

Mark carried the suitcase with the hundred thousand dollars in crisp new greenbacks and they quit the *Anna Two*. No other boats were in sight as they pulled away in the softness of the late afternoon calm.

Mark had brought a little of the white powder with him to show Angie, but she didn't believe the powder was cocaine.

"How do you know for sure?" she asked.

Mark took a small kit from his bag and showed her. It was Marquis test kit, and contained a three-inch-square porcelain spot plate and two small plastic vials with eye-droppers in the top.

"Take some of the powder and put in the cupped holes on the white plate," Mark told her. She did. "Now put five drops from bottle *A* on it."

Angie did; then Mark had her do the same with liquid from bottle *B*.

"Ugg, that smells awful," she said. But the drops went on and the white plate held the liquid on some of the white powder. Slowly the powder dissolved in the liquids and turned purple.

"That's sulphuric acid you put on first, and formaldehyde in the smelly bottle. If the material turns purple it's a hallucinating drug, heroin, cocaine. If it turns orange-brown, it's an amphetamine."

"So it's the real stuff?"

"Right, and the only high it's going to give might be to a stray jellyfish or two," Mark said, as the last of the powder fell into the sea.

In the Chris Craft Mark looked around. "Where's that seaman we left you with?" Mark asked. "The one I darted when he came aboard?"

"Him? Oh, he convinced me he was just a sailor, had papers to prove it, and really didn't want the job. So I gave him twenty dollars and put him off on Long Island. He said he could hitchhike back to town."

Mark rubbed his face with one hand. It might be just as well. He used the boat's radio and raised the Coast Guard, reporting a fishing boat adrift about a mile off Gallups Island, then signed off without identifying himself. They cruised slowly around George's Island until Mark saw the white Coast Guard cutter slicing through the water toward the *Anna Two*.

"Let's go home," Mark said.

Chapter Fourteen

TEST BY FIRE

It was after dark by the time Angie made the calls. When she was satisfied, they transferred Don Carlo Rossi to the private clinic she had selected. He was registered as Joseph Marshall, and ten thousand dollars was paid, cash in advance, against charges for his care. Angie stayed at the clinic to be sure he got settled in.

Mark and Tony left the rented van on a side street and drove the car back to the motel. They worked on cans of beer as they went over the layout of the safe house where Monica and little Tony were being held.

Mark tossed down the pencil and stretched. "It should work," he said, walking around the room.

"It's got to work," Tony said. "Look, I won't carry a weapon, I just won't, never again."

Mark watched the man carefully. Was he blowing? Could he be relied on for this one last mission? Mark plotted it out swiftly and came to the conclusion that Tony would hold up for what he had in mind. He would because during this attack the lives of his family would be in the balance.

"Tony, you don't need a weapon. It's got to work. There's no way they could win without one hell of a lot of firepower, and I'm sure they won't want to use that with all those people running around. This isn't their hard site, or their GHQ. It's just a safe house. Five, maybe six soldiers are there, now that they know I'm in town. No more. Two loads of darts and I should have everything wrapped up."

"Let's go," Tony said.

It was a little after ten o'clock when they split up. Mark dropped Tony two blocks below the safe house. Tony walked toward the gate of the private drive as Mark wheeled the car around three blocks. He came at the target from the other side, at the same place where he had taken the fall after talking to Monica on that first night, which now seemed weeks ago.

This time he would not use the rope. He planned to attack the cliff to the left of the target, where there was no overhang. There were also plenty of handholds and toeholds here to help him up the nearly vertical cliff. By cutting down on mechanical aids such as a rope, he was also cutting down on apparatus that could fail.

Mark moved to the cliff and began his climb. He wore dark blue, skin-tight pants, rubber-soled shoes, a tight-fitting pullover, and a slender belt with several pouches hanging from it. This had to be a silent mission all the way.

He tested the hard sandstone, found it more reliable than he remembered, and began moving upward.

No sensible hard-rock climber would take on this cliff without some good drive bolts and tough nylon life lines, but Mark utilized his remarkable sense of balance and knowledge of cracks and crevices and moved up the wall almost as if he were climbing a chain-link fence.

Five minutes after he had begun, he edged over the top and stared directly at a Mafioso guard, who had stepped to the edge of the cliff to flip a snubbed-out cigarette into the canyon. Mark shot him with Ava. The man dropped and writhed in pain. He had no time to draw his weapon or even cry out an alarm. Mark slid behind a privet hedge and watched the whole lighted back yard. No one else was there. No one came to see why the guard had decided to take a nap. The guard would be out for at least ten minutes.

Two blocks away, Tony slid into the shrubbery next to the sidewalk and floated from cover to cover as he advanced on the gate. He had learned to move swiftly and silently through the jungle when he had escaped from New Guinea. It was something you never forgot.

Tony stopped in the deep shadows near the gate. The guard was bored. Twice he had taken his gun from its hip holster and checked the rounds. He nodded off once, but Tony couldn't rely on his going to sleep. The fence was eight feet high and chain link. There was no way he could climb it silently. Tony found two good-sized rocks, and when the guard turned, he threw both into the brush on the far side of the drive, across from the small guard house. The man came alert at once, stormed from the guard post and across the road, looking in the bushes with his flashlight.

Tony ran as soon as the guard did. By the time the guard's flashlight was poking into the bushes, Tony had rounded the open gate, and in three long strides he faded behind a thick tree and let his breathing return to normal. The guard went back to the shack and used the phone, then began playing a game of tic tac toe with himself. He was losing.

Tony moved upward along the winding, dark drive. Once away from the shack, he moved faster, jogging until he was within fifty yards of the house. He found the spot he wanted, where dry grass and leaves had accumulated just off the drive, next to a small evergreen tree. Tony used one of the phosphorous grenades Mark had given him, covering it with leaves in the tall, dry grass, then pulling the pin. Tony ran. The explosion was like a firecracker, and Tony glued himself against a big maple tree and didn't move. The burning phosphorous quickly ignited the grass and leaves and within thirty seconds had touched off two evergreens. He could see the fire moving through the dry grass, a light wind blowing it toward the house.

Tony hit the paving and ran full tilt for the guard house.

"Fire! Fire!" Tony screeched as he came within sight of the guard. "Use your damn phone, shithead!" Tony yelled at the guard. "Get the fire department out here. It's blowing toward the house. *Do it now!*"

The guard had drawn his gun, but now confusion engulfed him. He pushed the weapon back in leather and reached for the phone, but he could only call the house. As the guard tried to figure out what to do, Tony slid past him, out the gate, and vanished into the heavy shadows. Now all he could do was wait.

In the privet hedge at the lip of the canyon, Mark smelled the smoke before he saw or heard anything. Grass smoke isn't something that gets by a mountain man or a desert-trained outdoorsman. Mark knew it was time for action. The unconscious guard hadn't moved or been found. Mark edged through a hedge, ran along the yard to the rearmost part of the house, and planted a phosphorous fire bomb. He settled a second against the tinder-dry underside of the old home and pulled both pins; then he ran back to the privet hedge.

Mark had explained to Tony that once phosphorous starts to burn, there is almost no way to put it out. The best method of combatting it is to help it burn itself up faster. No one in the place happened to know that when the flames began chewing away at the rear of the safe house on the cliff. Four minutes elapsed on Mark's watch before he heard sirens. Someone must have called about Tony's brush fire. Now they would have another problem.

The Penetrator sensed new lights snap on around the old house, as they tried for more security. A roving guard came around the back corner and saw the fire and rushed inside to give the alarm.

It was a forty-foot shot to the spot where the

witnesses came to look at the fire. Mark put the first three to sleep with Ava's darts, but missed the fourth, who moved in that split second before Mark fired.

He heard more sirens now. Angry voices shouted, and Mark made his move, running to the fence, hoisting up to the roof, and moving to the third floor the same way he had gained entry the first time. The third floor was still in shadows as Mark lifted the window and rolled into the room. A child cried. Footsteps sounded near the room. A dull light came on outside it.

Mark spoke before the woman came into the child's room.

"Monica, Tony says it's time now. You're both to come with me."

She stepped past the door, saw him, and nodded.

"First let me dress."

"No, it's better this way. Hurry. I'll bring the boy."

They could smell smoke as they went down the first stairs. A man ran past, ignoring them. At the start of the next flight of steps a guard materialized.

"What the hell? You're supposed to be upstairs."

"There's a fire; I smelled smoke," Monica said. By the time she said it Mark had shot the man with a silent dart and he fell moaning on the floor.

They moved downward, the smoke smell stronger.

At the foot of the steps Mark pointed at the front door. Most of the lights were on now. Two more men came from the side. Mark fired twice, then again, until the second man stumbled and fell. Mark slid a fresh pack of darts into the tranquilizer gun and they walked to the front door.

Just outside two men stood with rifles. A third was shouting at them.

"I don't give a damn what you think, Martello. Orders say we stay here, and keep our guests here." He turned.

Mark put a dart in his belly, shot the second man in the groin, and the third he clubbed twice on the neck with the side of his flat hand, putting the gunman down with a broken collar bone.

Below, the flames burned brighter. A ball of fire rushed up an evergreen, exploding as it went, only to burn itself out at the top where the rosin-laden needles ended. Fire crept along both sides of the drive, moving toward the house.

A fire bell clanged as a pumper truck worked its way up the drive, searchlights probing into the darkness.

A bullhorn boomed in front of them.

"The house has caught. Get a line up there; *C* section move!"

A moment later six men rushed by, tugging an empty hose.

"Get a tanker up the hill, on the double. The whole damn house could go. Bring in another line. Call in that second alarm; we need more people!"

Mark and Monica walked to one side of the driveway, heading for the darkness around a four-car garage that had been built fifty yards from the house and much later. They stepped into the shadows and Mark felt a gun in his back.

"One move and you're dead," a voice said. Mark became a pillar of steel. "I don't know who the hell you are, but the lady and the brat stay."

"Big Mike said bring them out, so I take them," Mark said. "Ain't you heard? The rap's out that the real Tony is in town and we got to make it look natural."

It was enough logic to cause the man with the gun to relax for a fraction of a second. Mark spun so fast the man never realized what had happened until Mark's hand chopped viciously down on the gun wrist. The weapon went off, ripping a hole in Mark's thigh, drilling lead through tissue, muscle, skin, and pants leg. Mark almost fell. The gun jolted to the ground. Mark's follow-through with his left hand drove the side of his hard hand into the bridge of the gunman's nose; then he kicked upward, his steel-capped boot toe smashing scrotum and testes into a bloody mass of terrible pain. The man fell, and Mark caught Monica by the elbow and moved her and little Tony on through the darkness.

No one noticed the shot. Fire bells clanged; men ran with hoses. Mark and Monica and little Tony slipped unnoticed around the edge of the activity through the trees and walked along hoses toward the brush fire.

It was a nothing blaze. Mark had worked forest fires in hundred-foot-tall fir and pines. This was not even a bonfire. When the line of fire neared, they moved to the middle of the paved drive and ran past the flames into a smoking jungle of hoses and curses and men struggling to mop up the backbreaking afterburn.

No guard stood at the gate. They walked toward it,

past the fire scene, confident, sure they were home free. But just as they came to the small sentry box, a form stepped out of the shadows. Mark almost fired, but something about the size and shape of the man stopped his hand.

"Tony?" Mark called.

The form ran forward.

"Monica?"

"Tony? Is it really you? Oh, darling!"

Then he was holding both Monica and little Tony in his arms in the sudden glare of a fire truck which had just pulled in from the street.

"Okay, move it, buddy, we've got a fire to put out up there!" a voice bellowed from behind the headlight beams.

Tony didn't even hear the man.

EPILOGUE

Four days later Mark lay back on the big, soft sofa in the six-room suite on the top floor of the Ritz Carlton Hotel. He had just finished having lunch in his room.

That morning a doctor had come and changed the dressing on his leg wound, which was starting to heal nicely, and shouldn't even leave a scar.

Tony had set up the whole thing, and was picking up the tab for it. A week's bed rest, he told Mark. Tony's own leg was mending too. The slug had been almost spent by the time it reached Tony and had only penetrated a little over an inch. A simple operation pulled it out. There was no police report filed on the bullet wound, and Tony was hard at work.

The day after they rescued his family, Tony had moved to the main Rossi mansion with a squad of police. The few Mafia soldiers remaining there melted into the woodwork, most drifting south to hook up with other families. He never saw the actor who played the phony Tony.

Tony reestablished his rights and properties; then the tough part came—sorting out the legitimate from the mobster activities. Some elements were simple and quickly closed up. The Mafia fronts were tougher and harder to untangle.

Tony said a battery of lawyers from outside the firm were moving in to evaluate every corporation, every company. The legal brains said it might take a year to come up with a definite estimate on the whole thing. His legitimate business empire still would be worth about twenty million.

Don Carlo was hanging on. He was on dope all right, but it was morphine. He needed it to keep the pain down to just below the screaming level. By now he was addicted to it, but he could still talk and they were building up his strength. The doctors warned Angie that he could die at any time. The tumors were inoperable; nothing could stop them.

The Coast Guard raised hell about the *Anna Two* and the death aboard. They launched a widespread search for the killer.

Angie had spent most of each day with her father, but he told her to get out of there and do something, like get married, and give him some grandchildren.

Mark phoned the professor in California and had a talk. The old one was worried about some problem in

Atlanta. Mark had never been to Atlanta. Maybe the professor would find something else more important.

He looked up as the doorbell sounded. Then the door opened, and he expected the maid or bellhop for the lunch tray. It was Angie.

"Now this is style," she said, coming in and dropping a light sweater on a chair. She wore a softly elegant white blouse that looked simple but must have cost a bundle.

"You have all the comforts of home. Lots of service, a color TV to while away your recuperation time, a soft couch to sit on, and a wonderful view of picturesque, historic Boston." Angie giggled and sat down beside him.

Mark pulled her close and kissed her lips. She snuggled down against him.

"Is this a good time to talk?"

He shook his head.

"I want to talk anyway."

"Gently; I'm recuperating."

"You're freeloading. That's what you're doing. One little favor you do a Rossi and you'll probably be around our necks till it snows, soaking up the good life."

"True."

"Okay, you win. I won't get serious. I absolutely won't get serious. I figured that out about you that very first day, you know, when I tried to shoot you. Wow! I told myself. Look, self, I said. Here is a ten on the scale of one to ten in fantastic men. A real live ten! Careful, I warned self. Why is he still floating around unclaimed if he's a ten? And then I kissed you and I knew: never serious. Kiss and mess around and tell. So I'm not serious either. We're two of a kind."

"Except you're rich, ten million rich."

"So are you. That suitcase of yours is bulging with two hundred and twenty thousand dollars. That's rich."

"That's company money, for the cause."

"You're the company."

"So?"

"So are you ever going to kiss me again? I didn't come up here to talk about your damned money."

He kissed her once, then again. After that she began unbuttoning his shirt.

The phone rang.

"Oh, no, not again," she wailed.

He picked it up and said hello.

"Mark, this is Willard Haskins. Remember that talk we had about Atlanta? How fast can you get down there? It looks like a real bad one."

"What kind of a problem, Professor?"

"We have checked it as far as we can, Mark, and there seems little doubt that there is something extremely peculiar going on in Atlanta and environs. However, we have no way of ascertaining precisely what it is from our position. First reports indicate some type of a modern-day vigilante group. Then it looked more like a gang of freebooters. It could also be some type of a for-hire gang of killers."

Mark frowned. "Didn't we have some kind of input on that about a month ago?"

"True, Mark, the tape recording from our good friend in Justice. We had another of them today, rather startling."

"And I bet you have your usual 'interesting packet of background materials' ready for my perusal."

"Exactly, Mark. I couldn't have put it more succinctly. Yes. Now where shall I airmail them?"

Mark told him the James Farris name at the Ritz Carlton.

"And do phone me after you've studied the lot. We may have something more on this by then. How is the leg?"

"About ninety percent. In another two days it should be back to normal."

"Good. Now keep in touch."

They said goodbye and Angie frowned at him.

"Another two days? You're crazy! That leg won't be normal for at least two or three weeks."

"It'll be good enough if I have to stress it. Now where were we?"

She grinned and began unbuttoning his shirt again, then reached for his belt. Mark grabbed her and flipped open the top button of her blouse.

"But, Mark, what about Atlanta?" she said in mock surprise.

Mark scowled, kissed her softly. "I don't care who Atlanta is," Mark said. "She'll just have to get in line and wait her turn like the other girls."

THE PENETRATOR

by Lionel Derrick

Mark Hardin. Discharged from the army, after service in Vietnam. His military career was over. But *his* war was just beginning. His reason for living and reason for dying became the same—to stamp out crime and corruption wherever he finds it. He is deadly; he is unpredictable; and he is dedicated. He is The Penetrator!

Read all of him in:

Order		Title	Book No.	Price
_____	# 1	THE TARGET IS H	P236	$ .95
_____	# 2	BLOOD ON THE STRIP	P237	$ .95
_____	# 3	CAPITOL HELL	P318	$ .95
_____	# 4	HIJACKING MANHATTAN	P338	$ .95
_____	# 5	MARDI GRAS MASSACRE	P378	$ .95
_____	# 6	TOKYO PURPLE	P434	$1.25
_____	# 7	BAJA BANDIDOS	P502	$1.25
_____	# 8	THE NORTHWEST CONTRACT	P540	$1.25
_____	# 9	DODGE CITY BOMBERS	P627	$1.25
_____	#10	THE HELLBOMB FLIGHT	P690	$1.25

TO ORDER

Please check the space next to the book/s you want, send this order form together with your check or money order, include the price of the book/s and 25¢ for handling and mailing to:

PINNACLE BOOKS, INC. / P.O. Box 4347
Grand Central Station / New York, N.Y. 10017

☐ **CHECK HERE IF YOU WANT A FREE CATALOG**

I have enclosed $_____ check_____ or money order_____ as payment in full. No C.O.D.'s

Name_____

Address_____

City_____ State_____ Zip_____

(Please allow time for delivery)

ALL NEW DYNAMITE SERIES

THE DESTROYER

by Richard Sapir & Warren Murphy

CURE, the world's most secret crime-fighting organization created the perfect weapon—Remo Williams—man programmed to become a cold, calculating death machine. The super man of the 70s!

Order		Title	Book No.	Price
_____	# 1	Created, The Destroyer	P361	$1.25
_____	# 2	Death Check	P362	$1.25
_____	# 3	Chinese Puzzle	P363	$1.25
_____	# 4	Mafia Fix	P364	$1.25
_____	# 5	Dr. Quake	P365	$1.25
_____	# 6	Death Therapy	P366	$1.25
_____	# 7	Union Bust	P367	$1.25
_____	# 8	Summit Chase	P368	$1.25
_____	# 9	Murder's Shield	P369	$1.25
_____	#10	Terror Squad	P370	$1.25
_____	#11	Kill or Cure	P371	$1.25
_____	#12	Slave Safari	P372	$1.25
_____	#13	Acid Rock	P373	$1.25
_____	#14	Judgment Day	P303	$1.25
_____	#15	Murder Ward	P331	$1.25
_____	#16	Oil Slick	P418	$1.25
_____	#17	Last War Dance	P435	$1.25
_____	#18	Funny Money	P538	$1.25
_____	#19	Holy Terror	P640	$1.25
_____	#20	Assassins Play-Off	P708	$1.25
_____	#21	Deadly Seeds	P760	$1.25
_____	#22	Brain Drain	P805	$1.25
_____	#23	Child's Play	P842	$1.25
_____	#24	King's Curse	P879	$1.25

the Executioner

The gutsiest, most exciting hero in years. Imagine a guy at war with the Godfather and all his Mafioso relatives! He's rough, he's deadly, he's a law unto himself — nothing and nobody stops him!

THE EXECUTIONER SERIES by DON PENDLETON

Order		Title	Book #	Price
_____	# 1	WAR AGAINST THE MAFIA	P401	$1.25
_____	# 2	DEATH SQUAD	P402	$1.25
_____	# 3	BATTLE MASK	P403	$1.25
_____	# 4	MIAMI MASSACRE	P404	$1.25
_____	# 5	CONTINENTAL CONTRACT	P405	$1.25
_____	# 6	ASSAULT ON SOHO	P406	$1.25
_____	# 7	NIGHTMARE IN NEW YORK	P407	$1.25
_____	# 8	CHICAGO WIPEOUT	P408	$1.25
_____	# 9	VEGAS VENDETTA	P409	$1.25
_____	#10	CARIBBEAN KILL	P410	$1.25
_____	#11	CALIFORNIA HIT	P411	$1.25
_____	#12	BOSTON BLITZ	P412	$1.25
_____	#13	WASHINGTON I.O.U.	P413	$1.25
_____	#14	SAN DIEGO SIEGE	P414	$1.25
_____	#15	PANIC IN PHILLY	P415	$1.25
_____	#16	SICILIAN SLAUGHTER	P552	$1.25
_____	#17	JERSEY GUNS	P328	$1.25
_____	#18	TEXAS STORM	P353	$1.25
_____	#19	DETROIT DEATHWATCH	P419	$1.25
_____	#20	NEW ORLEANS KNOCKOUT	P475	$1.25
_____	#21	FIREBASE SEATTLE	P499	$1.25
_____	#22	HAWAIIAN HELLGROUND	P625	$1.25
_____	#23	ST. LOUIS SHOWDOWN	P687	$1.25
_____	#24	CANADIAN CRISIS	P779	$1.25
_____	#25	COLORADO KILL-ZONE	P824	$1.25
_____	#26	ACAPULCO RAMPAGE	P868	$1.25

TO ORDER
Please check the space next to the book/s you want, send this order form together with your check or money order, include the price of the book/s and 25¢ for handling and mailing to:
PINNACLE BOOKS, INC. / P.O. BOX 4347
Grand Central Station / New York, N.Y. 10017
☐ **CHECK HERE IF YOU WANT A FREE CATALOG**
I have enclosed $_____ check_____ or money order_____ as payment in full. No C.O.D.'s.

Name_____

Address_____

City_____ State_____ Zip_____
(Please allow time for delivery.)   PB-38